Table Of Contents

    60 Year Deity 60太岁Marriage & Relationships 3
    The Ten Heaven Stems are: 3
    The Twelve Earth Branch are: 3
Chapter 1 : Jia Yang Wood 甲阳木: 3
    i) Jia Zi Day Master 甲子日元： 3
    ii) Jia Yin Day Master 甲寅日元： 3
    iii) Jia Chen Day Master 甲辰日元: 3
    iv) Jia Wu Day Master 甲午日元： 3
    v) Jia Shen Day Master 甲申日元: 3
    vi) Jia Xu Day Master 甲戌日元: 3
Chapter 2 : Yi Yin Wood 乙阴木: 3
    vii) Yi Chou Day Master 乙丑日元： 3
    viii) Yi Mao Day Master 乙卯日元: 3
    ix) Yi Si Day Master 乙巳日元: 3
    x) Yi Wei Day Master 乙未日元: 3
    xi) Yi You Day Master 乙酉日元: 3
    xii) Yi Hai Day Master 乙亥日元: 3
Chapter 3 : Bing Yang Fire 丙阳火: 3
    xiii) Bing Zi Day Master 丙子日元： 3
    xiv) Bing Yin Day Master 丙寅日元: 3
    xv) Bing Chen Day Master 丙辰日元: 3
    xvi) Bing Wu Day Master 丙午日元: 3
    xvii) Bing Shen Day Master 丙申日元: 3
    xviii) Bing Xu Day Master 丙戌日元: 3
Chapter 4 : Ding Yin Fire 丁阴火： 3
    xix) Ding Chou Day Master 丁丑日元: 3
    xx) Ding Mao Day Master丁卯日元: 3
    xx.i) Ding Si Day Master 丁巳日元: 3
    xx.ii) Ding Wei Day Master丁未日元: 3
    xx.iii) Ding You Day Master丁酉日元: 3
    xx.iv) Ding Hai Day Master丁亥日元: 3
Chapter 5 : Wu Yang Earth 戊阳土: 3

xx.v) Wu Zi Day Master 戊子日元: 3

xx.vi) Wu Yin Day Master 戊寅日元: 3

xx.vii) Wu Chen Day Master 戊辰日元: 3

xx.viii) Wu Wu Day Master 戊午日元: 3

xx.ix) Wu Shen Day Master 戊申日元: 3

xxx) Wu Xu Day Master 戊戌日元: 3

Chapter 6 : Yi Yin Earth 已阴土 : 3

xxx.i) Yi Chou Day Master 已丑日元: 3

xxx.ii) Yi Mao Day Master 已卯日元: 3

xxx.iii) Yi Si Day Master 已巳日元: 3

xxx.iv) Yi Wei Day Master 已未日元: 3

xxx.v) Yi You Day Master 已酉日元: 3

xxx.vi) Yi You Day Master 已酉日元: 3

Chapter 7 : Geng Yang Metal 庚阳金 3

xxx.vii) Geng Zi Day Master 庚子日元: 3

xxx.viii) Geng Yin Day Master 庚寅日元: 3

xxx.ix) Geng Chen Day Master 庚辰日元: 3

XL) Geng Wu Day Master 庚午日元: 3

XL.i) Geng Shen Day Master 庚申日元: 3

XL.ii) Geng Xu Day Master 庚戌日元: 3

Chapter 8 : Xin Yin Metal 辛阴金 3

XL.iii) Xin Chou Day Master 辛丑日元: 3

XL.iv) Xin Chou Day Master 辛丑日元: 3

XL.v) Xin Si Day Master 辛巳日元: 3

XL.vi) Xin Wei Day Master 辛未日元: 3

XL.vii) Xin You Master 辛酉日元: 3

XL.viii) Xin Hai Master 辛亥日元: 3

Chapter 9 : Ren Yang Water 壬阳水 3

XL.ix) Xin Si Master 辛巳日元: 3

L) Ren Yin Day Master 壬寅日元: 3

L.i) Ren Chen Day Master 壬辰日元: 3

L.ii) Ren Wu Day Master 壬午日元: 3

L.iii) Ren Shen Day Master 壬申日元: 3

L.iv) Ren Xu Day Master 壬戌日元: 3

Chapter 10 : Gui Yin Water 癸 阴水 3

L.v) Gui Chou Day Master 癸丑日元: 3

    L.vi) Gui Mao Day Master 癸卯日元: 3
    L.vii) Gui Si Day Master 癸巳日元: 3
    L.viii) Gui Wei Day Master 癸未日元: 3
    L.ix) Gui You Day Master 癸酉日元: 3
    LX) Gui You Day Master 癸酉日元: 3
Chapter 11 : Peach Blossom 3
    i) From the main door directions: 3
    ii) From the Day Master Wealth (for male) / Authority star (for lady): 3
    iii) From the Day Master spouse palace: 3
    iv) From Year of birth: 3
    Year of Birth Peach Blossom Direction 3
    v) From natal chart Year and/or Day Branch： 3
Conclusion 3
Introduction 1

Introduction

In all Chinese divinations method, the "Day Master 日元" is **you**! It represent you and your relationship with all other Elements and Pillar as well as the Current Year and 10 Year Luck Cycle which reveal events and happenings.

The Day Master is the Day Pillar Stem and Branch, which is the **day** you are born and it will determine your life destiny path.

Understanding one's Day Master goes a long way in improving your life as well as avoiding disasters and/or calamities, as well as hidden sickness (knowing these and seeking treatments early as prevention better than cures).

Getting into the suitable career/business will ensure more success and attaining higher position/status.

Knowing your suitable life partner will ensure a more blissful and long lasting happy family.

60 Year Deity 60太岁
Marriage & Relationships

Ancient Chinese Sages paired the 10 Heaven Stems and 12 Earth Branch to form the 60 Year Deities (60 太岁) to denotes Year, Month, Day and Hour as well as the 10 Gods stars 十神星. These 10 Gods stars are very important in reading your lifepath destiny.

These 60 Year Deities 60 太岁 are :

1	2	3	4	5	6	7	8	9	10	Star of Void
Jia 甲 Zi 子 1924/04/44	Yi 乙 Chou 丑 1925/05/45	Bing 丙 Yin 寅 1926/06/46	Ding 丁 Mao 卯 1927/07/47	Wu 戊 Chen 辰 1928/08/48	Ji 己 Si 巳 1929/09/49	Geng 庚 Wu 午 1930/00/50	Xin 辛 Wei 未 1931/01/51	Ren 壬 Shen 申 1932/02/52	Gui 癸 You 酉 1933/03/53	Xu 戌 Hai 亥
Jia 甲 Xu 戌 1934/04/54	Yi 乙 Hai 亥 1935/05/55	Bing 丙 Zi 子 1936/06/56	Ding 丁 Chou 丑 1937/07/57	Wu 戊 Yin 寅 1938/08/58	Ji 己 Mao 卯 1939/09/59	Geng 庚 Chen 辰 1940/00/60	Xin 辛 Si 巳 1941/01/61	Ren 壬 Wu 午 1942/02/62	Gui 癸 Wei 未 1943/03/63	Shen 申 You 酉
Jia 甲 Shen 申 1944/04/64	Yi 乙 You 酉 1945/05/65	Bing 丙 Xu 戌 1946/06/66	Ding 丁 Hai 亥 1947/07/67	Wu 戊 Zi 子 1948/08/68	Ji 己 Chou 丑 1949/09/69	Geng 庚 Yin 寅 1950/00/70	Xin 辛 Mao 卯 1951/01/71	Ren 壬 Chen 辰 1952/02/72	Gui 癸 Si 巳 1953/03/73	Wu 午 Wei 未
Jia 甲 Wu 午 1954/04/74	Yi 乙 Wei 未 1955/05/75	Bing 丙 Shen 申 1956/06/76	Ding 丁 You 酉 1957/07/77	Wu 戊 Xu 戌 1958/08/78	Ji 己 Hai 亥 1959/09/79	Geng 庚 Zi 子 1960/00/80	Xin 辛 Chou 丑 1961/01/81	Ren 壬 Yin 寅 1962/02/82	Gui 癸 Mao 卯 1963/03/83	Chen 辰 Si 巳
Jia 甲 Chen 辰 1964/04/84	Yi 乙 Si 巳 1965/05/85	Bing 丙 Wu 午 1966/06/86	Ding 丁 Wei 未 1967/07/87	Wu 戊 Shen 申 1968/08/88	Ji 己 You 酉 1969/09/89	Geng 庚 Xu 戌 1970/00/90	Xin 辛 Hai 亥 1971/01/91	Ren 壬 Zi 子 1972/02/92	Gui 癸 Chou 丑 1973/03/93	Yin 寅 Mao 卯
Jia 甲 Yin 寅 1974/04/54	Yi 乙 Mao 卯 1975/05/55	Bing 丙 Chen 辰 1976/06/56	Ding 丁 Si 巳 1977/07/57	Wu 戊 Wu 午 1978/08/58	Ji 己 Wei 未 1979/09/59	Geng 庚 Shen 申 1980/00/10	Xin 辛 You 酉 1981/01/11	Ren 壬 Xu 戌 1982/02/12	Gui 癸 Hai 亥 1983/03/13	Zi 子 Chou 丑

The Ten Heaven Stems are:

Jia 甲	Yang Wood
Yi 乙	Yin Wood
Bing 丙	Yang Fire
Ding 丁	Yin Fire
Wu 戊	Yang Earth
Yi 己	Yin Earth
Geng 庚	Yang Metal
Xin 辛	Yin Metal
Ren 壬	Yang Water
Gui 癸	Yin Water

The Twelve Earth Branch are:

Yin 寅	Yang Wood	Tiger 虎
Mao 卯	Yin Wood	Rabbit 兔
Chen 辰	Yang Earth	Dragon 龙
Si 巳	Yin Fire	Snake 蛇
Wu 午	Yang Fire	Horse 马
Wei 未	Yin Earth	Goat 羊
Shen 申	Yang Metal	Monkey 猴
You 酉	Yin Metal	Cockerel 鸡
Xu 戌	Yang Earth	Dog 狗
Hai 亥	Yin Water	Pig 猪
Zi 子	Yang Water	Rat 鼠
Chou 丑	Yin Earth	Cow 牛

Chapter 1 :
Jia Yang Wood 甲阳木:

Jia甲 a Yang Wood, its bagua location at Zhen 震 at the East.

It denote Thunder Wood, flourishes in Spring. Jia Wood required the Metal energies to make it useful (using metal instructments to shape the wood into furnitures etc).

In astrology it denote Mars planet.

At the <u>Heaven stem</u> it denote Dragon dance of the Thunder claps.

It also denote

i) Sour taste;

ii) tall, growth;

iii) a benefactor, charitable person;

iv) a refined reputable person;

v) a leader;

vi) in body part, it denotes the liver and gall;

vii) a straight-forward and firm person.

At <u>Earth hidden stem</u> it represent the Tiger. Hai亥 have hidden stem Jia Wood. So what is the tiger in water? Its the crocodile.

It also denote a person able to bear heavy responsibility.

It also denote:

i) a tall tree;

ii) a road;

iii) a bridge;

iv) a stair, an elevator, a lift;

v) lamppost, telephone post;

vi) a chimney;

vii) tree trunk (dead wood);

viii) pillar, beam, huge wooden furniture.

In **people** it denote a leader, patriarch, leading role, role model, elder sibling, chairperson, doctor, court judge, a gentlemen, laborer.

In **nature/temperament** it denote energetic, robust, honest, upright, positive, proactive.

In **body parts** it denote the head, liver, gall, gall bladder, the face, limbs, beard, brain, numbness, hair and nails.

In **things/objects** it denote politics, agriculture and forestry, construction building industry.

In **plants/vegetations** it denote Pine tree, Cypress tree, betel palm, coconut tree, lychee fruits, hawthorn tree, bamboo, forage grass.

In **animals** it denote birds, lion, tiger, leopard, deer, snake, lizard etc.

In **utensil/objects** it denote Drum, flute, musical instruments, vibrator, crane, club/staff, farming tools, vehicles etc.

i) Jia Zi Day Master 甲子日元 :

	Year	Month	Day Master	Hour
Heaven Stem			**Jia 甲**	
Earth Branch			**Zi 子**	
Hidden Stem			癸-DR	

This Day Pillar is termed "Wooden Rat Day 木鼠日".

The Day Branch represent the spouse palace. As Zi 子 Water produce Jia Wood, it indicated the spouse are supportive and caring.

This hidden stem Zi 子 is this person Direct Resource star which is Mother star, thus this person is likely to have their mother and elders support too.

The spouse star is a Peach Blossom star, thus this person is very romantic.

Folks with Jia Zi Day Master 甲子日元 dislike being controlled.

i.i) Jia 甲 Wood said to Zi 子 Water : Don't think I don't know. I am not a child, Meaning : Jia Day Master people need to be respected.

i.ii) Zi said to Jia: Cool down. Don't be angry. I had done my best.

Meaning: Spouse need to understand the Day Master character and nature.

i.iii) The Day Master are normally elder than their spouse.

*** Folks with Jia Zi 甲子日元 Day Master are likely to meet future spouse during Year or month of the Rabbit兔, Horse马, Cockerel鸡 or Goat羊 年 月 or when their spouse palace encountered clash, conflict or harm 夫妻宫被审型破害.

ii) Jia Yin Day Master 甲寅日元 :

	Year	Month	Day Master	Hour
Heaven Stem			Jia 甲	
Earth Branch			Yin 寅	Yin 寅
Hidden Stem			甲-RW 丙-EG 戊-IW	甲-RW 丙-EG 戊-IW

This Day Pillar is termed " Wooden Tiger Day 树虎日".

This Day Master sat on the 'Lu禄' star and is rooted, indicate this person is energetic and healthy;

Hidden stem Bing Fire is the person Eating God star, indicating this person is likely to be wealthy and plumb;

Hidden stem Wu Earth is the person Indirect Wealth star indicated lack of communication skills (too self-centered).

Folks with this Day Master are likely to develop young, but old age is problematic.

Close kin relationship are poor. Marriage life also problematic.

Note: Lady with this Day Master (with such a strong Day Master energies) are likely to be detrimental to her husband 女命克夫。

Folks with Jia Yin Day Master 甲寅日元, love needed to be mutually respected. Extra-martial affairs are unacceptable.

Unfortunately, Jia Yin folks are born with the 'Lonely Phoenix Calamities star 孤鸾煞' in which wife and husband can't get along, indicated multi-marriage, if not separated or divorced the other party will die first.

Those Jia Yin Day Master born in the Yin hour 寅时, the likelihood (of this harmful star) is very high. Thus, when choosing birth date for baby, this date must be avoided at all cost.

i) In a male destiny: This guy needs to take care of his spouse health as after childbirth, his wife health will deteriorate.

ii) In a female destiny : Due to work commitment or other factors, frequently they don't have time for the husband.

iii) Jia Yin formed a forest, thus the couple are unlikely to stay together till old age (too sociable and have too many relationships, thus likely to be separated or divorce).

iv) Eight out of ten Jia Wood Day master folks will get involved in extra-martial affairs.

***Folks with Jia Yin 甲寅日元 Day Master are likely to meet their future spouse in the Year or month of Snake, Monkey or Pig蛇，侯，猪 年 月 or

when their spouse palace encountered clash, conflict or harm
夫妻宫被审型破害.

iii) Jia Chen Day Master 甲辰日元:

	Year	Month	Day Master	Hour
Heaven Stem			**Jia 甲**	
Earth Branch			**Chen 辰**	
Hidden Stem			已-DW 戊-IW 癸-DR	

This Day Pillar is termed "Wood Riding Dragon Hour木骑龙日".

Folks with this Day Master are opportunistic, doesn't want to be tied down but will keep to the working routines. They will not worry about daily needs. They are hardworking during middle age.

This Day Master sat on its 'wealth depository财库, thus they will likely lived a wealthy and honorable life.

Folks with Jia Chen Day Master 甲辰日元 are likely to be very careless during early life but will be wealthy during old age.

Furthermore, they must ensure their spouse have the puppy love feeling / affections.

Note: Chen辰had hidden stems Yi已 Wu戊 Gui癸；

Yi已 is the Day Master Direct Wealth star, indicating the spouse have a stable job, love family and wife as well as very careful with money;

Wu戊 is the Day Master Indirect Wealth star, indicated this person have strong business acumen and will always remember their loved one as they are very passionate folks;

　　Gui癸 is the Day Master Direct Resource star, indicated love for learning and authoritative power.

　　Thus Jia Chen folks spouse are usually very highly educated, smart and elegant.

i) Jia Chen folks' marriage life are not easily appreciated by other.

ii) If your spouse is a Jia Chen Day Master, they are truly trustworthy, maybe they can't express their feelings. They truly loved their spouse.

***Folks with Jia Chen甲辰日元 Day Master are likely to meet their future spouse in the Year or month of Cow, Rabbit, Dragon or Dog 牛，兔，龙，狗年 or when their spouse palace encountered clash, conflict or harm 夫妻宫被审型破害.

iv) Jia Wu Day Master 甲午日元：

	Year	Month	Day Master	Hour
Heaven Stem			**Jia** 甲	
Earth Branch			**Wu** 午	
Hidden Stem			丁-HO 己-DW	

This Day Pillar is termed "Wood riding Horse Day 木骑马日".

Folks with this Day Master marriage life are likely to be problematic. They will likely live a laborious life of toil and hard-work.

Jia Wood Day Stem produce Day Branch Wu Fire, indicate this person will love the spouse. Hidden stem Ding Fire is a wealth producing source, thus likely to be wealthy.

Folks with Jia Wu Day Master 甲午日元 spouse had very strong Peach Blossom star property, indicating they are very likable, friendly and sociable because Wu午 is one of the four Peach Blossom star palace.

After marriage, the Jia Wu Day Master are likely to encounter extra-marital relationships. In the worst situation, they may bring their lover home!

Jia Wu Day Master success are usually due to the spouse support and influences. They success will come from their established trade/skills.

If the Jia Wu Day Master spouse is also a Wu午, then surely the Day Master success are due to the spouse support and influences.

***Folks with Jia Wu 甲午日元 Day Master are likely to meet their future spouse in the Year or month of Rat, Cow, Rabbit and Horse 鼠，牛，兔，马

年 月 or when their spouse palace encountered clash, conflict or harm 夫妻宫被审型破害.

v) Jia Shen Day Master 甲申日元:

	Year	Month	Day Master	Hour
Heaven Stem			**Jia** 甲	
Earth Branch			**Shen** 申	
Hidden Stem			庚-SK 壬-IR 戊-IW	

This Day Pillar is termed "Wooden Monkey Day 木猴日".

This is an ominous Day Master. Marriage life problematic as the spouse are likely to be too romantic and 'loose'.

The Day Master sat on its 'death' stage of life, indicating a difficult and laborious life.

Folks with Jia Shen Day Master 甲申日元 have very explosive hot temper and rashful, thus do not offend them. Shen 申 have hidden stems of Geng 庚 Ren 壬 Wu 戊 ;

Geng 庚 is the Day Master Seven Killing star 七杀星, indicating explosive hot temper;

Ren 壬 is the Day Master Indirect Resource star, indicating an introvert character but have special observance abilities;

Wu 戊 is the Day Master Indirect Wealth star, indicating this person is very sociable and have strong business acumen.

Male destiny folks with Jia Shen Day pillar are always controlled by their wife (Shen 甲 Metal controlled Jia 甲 Wood). They care more about their children and career/business.

Female destiny folks with Jia Shen Day pillar must not let their husband work in a female environment, such as night clubs, for their husband can easily have affairs with another women.

However, if there are Eating God or Hurting Officer stars or Resource stars around to suppress the Seven Killing stars, then the situations will be different.

***Folks with Jia Shen 甲申日元 Day Master folks are likely to meet their future spouse with those born in the Year or month of the Tiger, Snake or Pig 虎 蛇 猪 年 or when their spouse palace encountered clash, conflict or harm 夫妻宫被审型破害.

vi) Jia Xu Day Master 甲戌日元:

	Year	Month	Day Master	Hour
Heaven Stem			Jia 甲	
Earth Branch			Xu 戌	
Hidden Stem			戌-IW 辛-DA 丁-HO	

This Day Pillar is termed "Wooden Dog Day 木狗日".

Folks with this Day Master marriage life are problematic. This person is firm, unyielding, upright and honest.

They are too straight-forward and outspoken thus likely to get into troubles.

Folks with Jia Xu Day Master甲戌日元 spouse are very virtuous, kind and have good culinary skills.

Xu戌 is the Day Master Indirect Wealth star偏才星, thus they are very conscious of their money. However, Jia Xu Day Master folks truly loved their spouse and are faithful.

In a male destiny, any quarrels or disputes with spouse are caused by spouse problems or money matters.

Jia Xu Day Master folks spouse will always claim the husband success are due to her support or influences (Jia Wood can only grow in Xu Earth).

Jia Xu Day Master folks spouse will always fully support him even in term of monetary supports.

***Jia Xu Day Master folks are likely to meet their future spouse in the Year or month of the Cow, Dragon, Goat, Cockerel牛龙羊鸡年月 or when their spouse palace encountered clash, conflict or harm 夫妻宫被审型破害.

Chapter 2 :
Yi Yin Wood 乙阴木:

Yi乙 bagua location at Xun巽 at Southeast location.

Yi乙 is Yin阴 Wood. In astrology it denote the Moon apsis.

At the Heaven stem it denote Wind风, a formless energies. The changes caused by Yi Wood is very slow and hardly noticeable.

This is because Yi Wood can penetrate any crack in anything. It denotes a strong survival energies. Air have this energies, thus Yi Wood represent Wind, a moving air.

At the Earth hidden stem, it denote plants and flowers. It also denote sour taste, musical tones. It also denote pretentious affections, worldly affairs.

In human actions it denote crawling. Denote wife, hairs, eyebrow, ears, tongue, brain and mental state, blood systems, intestines, shoulder, limbs, things that can be bended. It also denote grassland, woodware.

In places it denote Botanical gardens, grassland, valley, flower shop, public orchard,etc.

In people it denote Scholar, virtuous person, monks/taoist priests, mother, sisters, wife, matchmaker, deputy etc.

In emotions/feeling it denote yielding and tenacious, tactful, adhesive and gentle.

In human body it denote liver, lacinmal gland (tear), hair, finger, thigh, limbs, nails, sense of smell, immortal soul, neck, nervous system, allergy, itchiness, brain etc.

In things/objects it denote Gardens, handicraft, middlemen, marriage, education, corrective education, printing & publication, settlement, negotiation, travel & tourism, tea, willow, thatch, dandelion, aromatic things, etc.

In animals it denote Mandarin ducks, turtledove, chicken/fowl, crane/stork, butterfly, dragonfly, moths, caterpillar, pangolin, snake, giraffes etc.

vii) Yi Chou Day Master 乙丑日元 :

	Year	Month	Day Master	Hour
Heaven Stem			**Yi** 乙	
Earth Branch			**Chou** 丑	
Hidden Stem			己-DW 癸-DR 辛-DA	

This Day Pillar is termed 'Grass Cow Day 草牛日".

Folks with this Day Master their spouse are pretty and attractive. Lady with this Day Master are likely to look manly.

Folks with Yi Chou Day Master 乙丑日元 has the qualities of flexibility and growth.

Thus, Yi Wood folks are good at adapting. Yi Wood is Yin Wood, associated with plants and flowers.

Yi Chou Day Master 乙丑日元 folks have many ideas but dare not work on it or do not know how to express it.

They often over-worried and thus put unnecessary pressure on themselves.

They can't control the other party.

Their spouse are usually very hot temper.

Thus, their children need detailed guidance and education.

Lady destiny with this Day Master likely to have problematic marriage life, indicating multi-marriage. It is advisable for these ladies to marry before sunrise, as this will break the marriage hoodoo.

They are also likely to be concerned and worried about their husband career/business.

In a Man destiny, their career/ business success are due to wife support and influences.

*** Folks with Yi Chou 乙丑日元 Day Master folks are likely to meet their future spouse born in the Year or month of Dragon, Horse, Goat, Dog 龙马羊狗 年月 or when their spouse palace encountered clash, conflict or harm 夫妻宫被审型破害.

viii) Yi Mao Day Master 乙卯日元:

	Year	Month	Day Master	Hour
Heaven Stem			**Yi** 乙	
Earth Branch			**Chou** 丑	
Hidden Stem			己-DW 癸-DR 辛-DA	

This Day Pillar is termed "Flower Rabbit Day 花兔日".

This is an auspicious Day Master. They have good literary skills and are good craftsman.

Folks with Yi Mao Day Master 乙卯日元 are very fond of people with the same interest and priorities. They are very sociable people.

People with this Day Master likes people with same interest, priorities and thinking.

Male destiny folks with this Day Master when their chart have 'Friend' star in their spouse palace are likely to divorce.

Female destiny with this Day Master are advised to marry late (better after 28 year old) or will also face the possibly of separation.

Female destiny people chart with strong Hurting Officers star 伤官星旺, their marriage seldom last long.

*** Folks with Yi Mao 乙卯日元 Day Master are likely to meet their future spouse born in the Year or Month of the Tiger, Monkey, Pig 虎 猴 猪 年 月 or when their spouse palace encountered clash, conflict or harm 夫妻宫被审型破害.

ix) Yi Si Day Master 乙巳日元:

	Year	Month	Day Master	Hour
Heaven Stem			Yi 乙	
Earth Branch			Si 巳	Si 巳
Hidden Stem			丙-EG 庚-DA 戊-DW	丙-EG 庚-DA 戊-DW

This Day Pillar is termed "Grass Snake Day 草蛇日".

This is an auspicious Day Master. Unfortunately, it is inflicted with the harmful 'Lonely Phoenix Calamities star孤鸾煞' thus marriage is problematic if not separated or divorced the other party will die first.

Yi Wood produces Si Fire indicated this person is intelligent but only benefit other people. A born fighter.

Folks with Yi Si Day Master 乙巳日元 are always giving, sacrificing for the spouse (Day stem Yi乙Wood produced Day Branch Si巳Fire).

Yi Si Day Master folks does not know how to make the first move to start a relationship.

Those Yi Si Day Master born in the Si hour巳时, the likelihood of having this harmful 'Lonely Phoenix Calamities star孤鸾煞' is very high. Thus when choosing birth date for baby, this date must be avoided at all cost.

The Si巳 Fire had hidden stems of Bing丙, Wu戊, Geng庚; Bing丙 is the Day Master Hurting Officer star伤官星, indicated the spouse will always scold the husband;

Wu戊 is the Day Master Direct Wealth star 正财星, indicating the spouse have a stable income job.

Geng庚 is the Day Master Direct Authority star 正官星, indicating this person is under the control of the spouse (Hurting Officer star suppress Direct Authority star 伤官星克正官星).

Yi Si Day Master folks, when the chart have strong Hurting Office stars官星旺, this person will likely face bankruptcy and/or have short life.

Hurting Officer star also denote rebellious nature. Thus, when your Hour pillar have Hurting Officer star, your children will be very rebellious and unfilial.

When your spouse palace (Day Branch) have Hurting Officer star, your wife will always scold you.

*** Folks with Yi Si乙巳日元 Day Master are likely to meet their future spouse born in the Year or Month of the Tiger, Monkey or Pig 虎 猴 猪 年 or when their spouse palace encountered clash, conflict or harm 夫妻宫被审型破害.

x) Yi Wei Day Master 乙未日元:

	Year	Month	Day Master	Hour
Heaven Stem			Yi 乙	
Earth Branch			Wei 未	
Hidden Stem			巳-IW 丁-EG 乙-Fr	

This Day Pillar is termed "Grass Goat Day 草羊日".

This is an auspicious Day Master as it sat on own 'wealth depository 财星入库, indicating a wealthy life. But this person like wealth too much thus are petty. However, this person will surely be wealthy when their chart encountered a clash/ conflict of the wealth star (Wei未), that is when the Current Year or 10 Year Luck Cycle enter the Cow Year 牛年.

Folks with Yi Wei Day Master乙未日元 does not like to be controlled.

In a male destiny, when this Yi Wei Day Master suddenly become rich, he need to control himself and take care of his family first and not spent lavishly on other people (especially on other females).

The spouse palace 巳Wei未have hidden stems of Yi巳 Ding丁 Yi乙 ;

Yi巳 is the Day Master Indirect Wealth star偏才星, indicating a ravish spender. They had not hesitation on entertaining friends (especially the opposite sex);

Ding丁 is the Day Master Eating God star食神星, indicating this person love foods and socializing;

Yi乙 is the Day Master 'Friend' star 比肩星, indicating this person is an extrovert. They care more about 'friends' then family member. Besides, they had very strong self ego. Lady with this Day Master will always control their spouse.

Furthermore, those with 'Friend' star at the spouse palace, this person must ensure to forget their past romantic affairs as they will surely seek their past 'lover' to reignite their relationship.

Lady with this Day Master will likely to have a blissful marriage life. They make good wife.

Folks with this Day Master, after their marriage must move out and stay on their own. If they stayed with their parents or close kins there'll be a lot of conflicts and disagreements.

*** Folks with this Yi Wei 乙未日元 Day Master are likely to meet their future spouse born in the Year or Month of the Rat, Cow or Dog 鼠 牛 狗

年月 or when their spouse palace encountered clash, conflict or harm 夫妻宫被审型破害.

xi) Yi You Day Master 乙酉日元:

	Year	Month	Day Master	Hour
Heaven Stem			**Yi** 乙	
Earth Branch			**You** 酉	**Si** 巳
Hidden Stem			辛-SK	丙-HO 戊-DW 庚-DA

This Day Pillar is termed "Flower Cockerel Day 花鸡日".

This is an ominous Day Master. Spouse have hot temper.

Main hidden stem Xin辛 the Seven Killing star denotes sickness and injuries;

Those born in Summer are treatable/ curable;

Those in Earth months (lunar 3rd, 6th, 9th, 12th month), may incur bodily injuries.

Generally, folks with this Day Master have short lifespan. Lady are pretty, attractive and romantic. May marry puppy love, not advisable. Better for these ladies to marry late (preferably after 28-year-old).

Folks with Yi You Day Master 乙酉日元 have very strong Peach Blossom star calamities (they will have too many complicated affection affairs).

Besides, You酉 have hidden stem Xin辛 the Day Master Seven

Killing star 七杀星, indicating this person will always be bullied by their spouse. It also indicated this person are very rashful and unable to control themselves. They will do thing without thinking.

(Note: When the Seven Killing star have support, separation or divorce is inadvertent).

But if this person is born in the month of Si巳 or Wu午 (Fire month), then this calamity will be lessened (Fire suppressed You酉 Metal).

*** Folks with Yi You 乙酉日元 Day Master are likely to meet their future spouse born in the Year or Month of the Rat, Rabbit, Dog or Cockerel 子 卯 狗 鸡 年 月 or when their spouse palace encountered clash, conflict or harm 夫妻宫被审型破害.

(note: Rat Rabbit and Cockerel are Peach Blossom stars)

xii) Yi Hai Day Master 乙亥日元:

	Year	Month	Day Master	Hour
Heaven Stem			Yi 乙	
Earth Branch			Hai 亥	
Hidden Stem			壬-DR 甲-RW	

This Day Pillar is termed "Flower Pig Day 花猪日".

Folks with this Day Master are generally intelligent. Difficult situations may suddenly have solution or improvement.

Males are likely to have a virtuous and devoted wife; Ladies are likely to very pretty and attractive and will have a good husband and are faithful and loyal wife.

Folks with Yi Hai Day Master 乙亥日元 are soft hearted and will give way easily even when they are in the right.

Yi Hai have hidden stems of Ren壬 and Jia甲; Ren壬 is the Day Master Direct Resource star正印星, indicating their spouse are highly educated and intelligent.

Jia甲 is the Day Master Rob Wealth star劫才星, indicating the spouse are firm and adventurous.

Female destiny with this Day Master are self-centered; They will do things their way.

Male destiny folks must learn to appreciate his spouse talent and skill. They will always let his wife take care of house-keeping.

Folks with this Day Master are introvert thus they will not make the first move in a relationship.

However, they like their spouse to love their family like own family.

*** Folks with Yi Hai 乙亥日元 Day Master are likely to meet their future spouse born in the Year or Month of the Tiger, Snake, Monkey or Pig虎蛇猴猪 年 月 or when their spouse palace encountered clash, conflict or harm 夫妻宫被审型破害.

Chapter 3 :
Bing Yang Fire 丙阳火:

Bing is the Sun energies, a fiery burning Fire, thus Bing in heaven is the Yang Fire. It can destroy everything!

Bing Fire also represent education and learning, the focus of a bright future.

In astrology it denote Jupiter planet.

At Heaven stem it denote lightnings.

At Earth Branch hidden stem it denote stove fire. It represented the radiant of the Yang Fire. When concentrated it denote fierce explosives nature; Denotes hot spicy taste; Denotes a man deep voice tone.

In general, it represent the Sun, round shape, red in color, rebellious, disturbance, blood, high fever, inflammation, window, higher level, swollen, blood flow, firecrackers, burning ambition, traffic lights, signals etc.

In land/properties it denote gateway, incense burner, palace, theater, grassland, court room, kiln/stove, entertainment hall etc.

In people it denote poet, hacker, missionary, pioneer, inspector, plaintiff, specialist, chemist, jockey, beautician, opththalmologist etc.

In emotion/feeling it represent firm looking on the outside but gentle internally.

In body parts it represent small intestines, eyes, shoulder, mole/speckle, blood pressure, inflammation, bloody cuts, burns, sunburn, infertility, abortions etc.

In things/objects it denote Official documents, information, gossips and quarrels, business gifts/donations, entertainment industry, airline industries, customer services etc.

In plants/vegetations it denote Angelica sinensis, peony, cockscomb flower, chili/hot pepper, lotus, maple etc. In animals it represent phoenix, magpies, sparrow, parrot, crab, shell/snails, fishes etc.

In tools/utensils it represent ceremonial robes, lamp/lantern, optical instruments, cosmetics, fax machine, copiers, TV, computer etc.

Other representation : Red color, purple color, Vermilion bird, Year Deity 'Rou Zhao' 柔兆太岁 etc.

xiii) Bing Zi Day Master 丙子日元 :

	Year	Month	Day Master	Hour
Heaven Stem			Bing 丙	
Earth Branch			Zi 子	
Hidden Stem			癸-DA	

This Day Pillar is termed "Fire Rat Day 火鼠日".

This is an auspicious Day Master. This is a 'Star of Yin Yang calamities 阴阳煞' Day Master. This star influences a person marriage and affection.

Lady is of Yin polarity and like Yang energies. When this lady encounter a strong Wu Wu 戊午 Fire energies, it is known as a 'Genuine' Yang energy.

Males are of Yang polarity and like Yin energies. When this man encounters a strong Bing Zi 丙子 Water energies, it is known as a 'Genuine' Yin energy.

When a Yin and Yang met in harmony, like when a male encounter Bing Zi

丙子 Water energies, he will meet many beautiful ladies in his life.

Like when a lady encounter Wu Wu 戊午 Fire energies, she will meet many handsome guys in her life.

When the Day Pillar have these energies, Male will marry a beautiful wife; while Lady will be married a handsome husband.

It is very detrimental when this Star shine with 'Yuan Chen star 元辰星' and/or 'Xian Chi star 咸池星'. They will lost their morals and become licentious.

Male with Wu Wu Day Pillar 戊 women. Female with is likely to elope.

Male with Wu Wu pillar 戊午, will likely have an affair with a married woman.   Female with Bing Zi Day Pillar 丙子 is likely to elope.

When a male have Wu Wu 戊午 Fire energies in his chart, he will married a loving wife. When a female have Bing Zi 丙子 Water energies, many guys will be chasing her (as a wife).

Bing 丙 Fire has the quality of upward climb. Fire fans out the quality of radiance, atmosphere and warmth. Bing Fire denotes the Sun Fire. It is a Yang Fire.

This Bing Zi Day Master 丙子日元 is very auspicious to a lady as it indicated she will be a good husband and live a blissful married life. However, they must stay away from the opposite sex as they will easily have affection with them.

Note: In a lady chart, if there are no Direct Authority star, Seven Killing star 七杀星 can also represent the spouse star.

However, Seven Killing stars in a lady chart also denote her 'lover'.

Thus lady chart with too many Seven Killing stars are rather 'loose' and thus will have problematic married life.

Direct Authority star 正官星 is a lady spouse star. People with many Direct Authority stars will not believe in Bazi divination as they think its superstition and they only believe in themselves.

In a male chart, folks with this Day Master are more conservative. Their thinking are pure and sincere, so the future spouse must not hide any secret from him. Thus people with this Day Master can live a long and happy married life.

Note: Folk's chart with a single Direct Authority star must have good education to be successful in life. Else they must have a special skill (no matter martial art or cultural skill).

Note: Folk's chart with a single Direct Authority star must have good education to be successful in life. Else they must have a special skill (no matter martial art or cultural skill).

No matter male or female, people with this Day Master must not waste their time on romances. This is because this Day Master Stem is Fire and Earth Branch is Water (fire will soon dry the water).

In Bing Zi Day Master, the Zi 子 is one of the four Peach Blossom star, indicating these people are romantic and have pleasant look (very likable look).

*** Folks with Bing Zi 丙子日元 Day Master are likely to meet their future spouse born in the Year or Month of the Rabbit, Horse, Cockerel or Goat 兔 牛 鸡 羊 年 月 or when their spouse palace encountered clash, conflict or harm 夫妻宫被审型破害.

xiv) Bing Yin Day Master 丙寅日元:

	Year	Month	Day Master	Hour
Heaven Stem			**Bing 丙**	
Earth Branch			**Yin 寅**	
Hidden Stem			甲-IR 丙-Fr 戊-EG	

This Day Pillar is termed "Fire Tiger Day 火虎日".

Folks with this Day Master have the quality of the Sun, splendor, brilliance and radiance. They are usually very intelligent.

Unfortunately it sat on Indirect Resource and Eating God star, which are not auspicious as these stars clashed.

Wu 戊 Earth 'Growth' stage of life at Yin 寅, thus the Eating God star energies are strong indicating this person is very intelligent. Very auspicious;

Born in early Winter and early Summer 生于夏至后冬至前, Wu 戊 Earth 'Growth' stage of life at Shen 申, Eating God star energies are 'weak', unable to produce 'wealth'.

Folks with Bing Yin Day Master 丙寅日元 have Bing Fire on top and Yin Wood below, indicating Yin Wood (the spouse star) will ignite the Bing Fire, indicating the passion is very strong at first sight.

Male destiny folks with this Day Master better to find a spouse that can help or support his career or business.

Furthermore, this guy temper will get bad after marriage.

Female destiny folks will benefit their husband with this Day Master as her energies will enhance her husband career or business 旺夫.

However, their health will deteriorate after each childbirth.

People with this Day Master are highly likely to have stroke (this could be due to their explosive temper). Furthermore, this Day Master have a 'Friend' star 比肩星 at the spouse palace indicating high likelihood or separation or divorce.

*** Folks with Bing Yin 丙寅日元 Day Master are likely to meet their future spouse born in the Year or Month of the Snake, Monkey or Pig 蛇 猴 猪 年 月 or when their spouse palace encountered clash, conflict or harm 夫妻宫被审型破害.

xv) Bing Chen Day Master 丙辰日元:

	Year	Month	Day Master	Hour
Heaven Stem			**Bing 丙**	
Earth Branch			**Chen 辰**	
Hidden Stem			戊-EG 乙-DR 癸-DA	

This Day Pillar is termed "Fire Dragon Day 火龙日".

This is an auspicious Day Master. These folks are usually very intelligent, witty.

Chen辰 are moist earth while Bing丙 is the Sun, sunlight shines over all things and produce lives. These folks are generally very intelligent and active.

Lady with this Bing Chen Day Master丙辰日元, after their marriage their health will deteriorate (Eating God star are produced by the Day Master, thus diminishing the Day Master energies, just like a women health deteriorate after giving birth). These ladies will also sacrifice (their freedom and wealth) to take care of her family.

They will love and take care of their husband.

They will likely love their daughter more than their husband (especially when the Eating God star energies are strong 食神星旺).

Male with this Day Master prefer their wife to maintenance their good look and attractiveness. After marriage, these guys will sacrifice (their freedom and wealth) to take care of his family.

Folks with this Day Master frequently 'structed' at their romancing stage of relationship, so lady must not co-habitat else they will lost their chastity.

Folks with this Day Master if there are Eating God 食神星 and/or Hurting Officer star伤官星 at the Hour pillar, it indicated they will enjoy their children care during old age.

People chart with this Day Master and when Chou丑 Mao卯 Chen辰 Xu戌 also appear in their chart, indicated these people are too romantic and can't control their emotions (thus will have too many romantic affairs).

*** Folks with Bing Chen 丙辰日元 Day Master are likely to meet their future spouse born in the Year or Month of the Cow牛 Rabbit兔 Dragon龙 Dog 狗 年 月 or when their spouse palace encountered clash, conflict or harm 夫妻宫被审型破害.

xvi) Bing Wu Day Master 丙午日元:

	Year	Month	Day Master	Hour
Heaven Stem			**Bing** 丙	
Earth Branch			**Wu** 午	
Hidden Stem			丁-RW 己-HO	

This Day Pillar is termed "Fire Horse Day 火马日".

This is an ominous Day Master. Folks with Bing Wu Day Master 丙午日元 have the harmful "Freak Error Calamities star 阴差阳错" as well as the harmful "'Lonely Phoenix Calamities star孤鸾煞';

"Freak Error Calamities star" denotes errors due to chance or random factors. It indicates the random factor why people cannot get along well. (阴差阳错yin cha yang cuo literary meant 'an accident arising from many causes'. This is a divination term coined by ancient masters to describe this type of calamities).

Chinese ancient saying: *"Lady encounter these, ancestors/ parents' relationship not close, brother/sisters-in-law too, husband family relationship also cold. Male encounter these, will move to in-law place, in-law gossip and dispute bring cold wars".*

When these calamities stars appeared at two or three pillar in the Month, Day or Hour pillars, the calamities is very serious.

However, if it only appear only in the Day Pillar, it is not so serious. The person will not have in-law family support. Even if the in-law is wealthy, it will be squander away. Over time it will cause enmity with in-law and separation.

People with this Stars are likely to have illegitimate children or siblings. Marriage are discussed during mourning and disagreements normally happen. Spouse cannot get along with parents. Cold wars within close kin. In work and career, they will let opportunities pass by and fail within sight of success.

"Lonely Phoenix Calamities star孤鸾煞" in which wife and husband can't get along, indicated multi-marriage, if not separated or divorced the other party will die first.

In a male destiny, after marriage they will find it hard to safe money (Rob Wealth star at spouse palace).

These folks need to establish a stable income career or business.

These guys also must avoid Peach Blossom attractions as it will bring their downfall (note Wu午 is one of the four Peach Blossom star 四大桃花星). It will also increase their separation/divorce chances.

Note: Children born on these double similar energies' day (such as Jia甲Wood Yin寅 Wood; Yi乙 Wood Mao卯 Wood; Bing丙 Fire Wu午 Fire; Ding丁 Fire Si巳 Fire; Geng庚 Metal Shen申 Metal; Xin辛Metal You酉 Metal; Ren壬 Water Zi子 Water; Gui癸 Water Chou丑 Water; will be problematic and difficult to raise.

In a lady destiny, after marriage she will face many disastrous calamities such as bankruptcy, husband demised, harm children or remarry (due to her strong Peach Blossom stars).

Most folks with Bing Wu Day Master have strong affinity with Buddhism.

Male destiny folks with Bing Wu Day Master must activate their 'Prolong life location 延年方' by placing a pixiu (a mythical animal that brings luck and wards off evil) while female destiny folks with this Day Master must keep their 'Five Ghost location 五鬼方' clean and tidy.

Note : Folks with Bing丙 Wu午 Day Master and when there's Wu午, the "Lonely Phoenix Calamities star 孤鸾煞' is activated in which wife and husband can't get along, indicated multi-marriage, if not separated or divorced the other party will die first. Those Bing Wu Day Master born in the Wu hour 午时, the likelihood is very high. Thus, when choosing birth date for baby, this date must be avoided at all cost.

*** Folks with Bing Wu 丙午日元 Day Master are likely to meet their future spouse born in the Year or Month of the Rat子 Cow牛 Rabbit兔 Horse马 年 月 or when their spouse palace encountered clash, conflict or harm 夫妻宫被审型破害.

xvii) Bing Shen Day Master 丙申日元:

	Year	Month	Day Master	Hour
Heaven Stem			**Bing 丙**	
Earth Branch			**Shen 申**	
Hidden Stem			庚-IW 壬-SK 戊-EG	

This Day Pillar is termed "Fire Monkey Day 火猴日".

Folks with this Day Master wife are strong headed but will care for the family.

The strong Seven Killing star indicated this person may have serious

41

sickness or injuries.

These folks are likely to live in hardship and poverty.

Male destiny folks with Bing Shen Day Master 丙申日元 are likely to be detrimental to spouse 男命克妻 (their wife likely to die after their marriage) as Bing Fire will melt Shen Metal. It also indicated their spouse health is poor.

When the Authority stars energizes are strong, this guy will be controlled by the wife. Lady destiny folks with this Day Master likely to have problematic married life. During their courtship beware not be cheated by a married man! Folks with this Day Master are hard working people but their married life are problematic (due to the two conflicting Elements). Note: Once these folks suddenly become wealthy, they will become nasty towards their family.

*** Folks with Bing Shen 丙申日元 Day Master are likely to meet their future spouse born in the Year or Month of the Tiger虎 Snake蛇 or Pig猪 年 月 or when their spouse palace encountered clash, conflict or harm 夫妻宫被审型破害.

xviii) Bing Xu Day Master 丙戌日元:

	Year	Month	Day Master	Hour
Heaven Stem			**Bing** 丙	
Earth Branch			**Xu** 戌	
Hidden Stem			戊-EG 辛-DW 丁-RW	

This Day Pillar is termed "Fire Dog Day 火狗日".

This Day Master sat on its own 'wealth depository 财库". Bing Fire blaze brightly, indicating these folks are intelligent and good looking.

Folks with Bing Xu Day Master 丙戌日元 are advised to marry late (preferably after 28 year of age). This is because this Day Master Bing Fire produced Xu Earth, indicating this Day Master will have to sacrifice to produce the Xu Earth (just like a mother, she sacrifices her health to give birth).

Lady with this Day Master frequently worried about her husband business or career. Unfortunately, they can't keep secret, too talkative.

Guy with this Day Master after their marriage, he must learn how to control himself and not have too many adventurous ideas to get rich.

Beware! Those with this Day Master and born at the Chen Hour (0700 to 0900 hour) 辰时;

Male destiny folks will harm their wife and/or children 男命伤妻克子;

While Lady destiny folks will harm husband and/or children 女命伤夫克子。

*** Folks with Bing Xu 丙戌日元 Day Master are likely to meet

their future spouse born in the Year or Month of the Cow牛 Dragon龙 Goat羊 Cockerel鸡 年 月 or when their spouse palace encountered clash, conflict or harm 夫妻宫被审型破害.

Chapter 4 :
Ding Yin Fire 丁阴火 :

Ding Yin Fire denote man-make fire, such as candle, small fire, street lightnings, lamps etc. Ding Fire denotes civilized ambiance. Its the pneuma of all living things.

In astrology it denote the Venus planet.

At the Heaven stem, it represents stars;

At the Earth Hidden stem, it represented candle/lamp lightnings (man make light).

In general, it represent red color things, flowers, small fire, smoke, it formed the auspicious 'Three Specialist' formation of Yi Bing Ding 三奇是乙丙丁' representing dreams (Ding dreams are the most auspicious), diced meat, dentist, acupuncture/moxibustion, volcanic eruption etc.

In things/objects it denote kin/stove, back door, small door, border, horse stable, kitchen etc.

In people it denote Female friends & peers, matchmaker, artist, actors, exam students, widow etc.

In emotions/feeling it denote devotion/ loyalty, soft & gentle, cool, does not conceded defeat, rebellious, introvert, stubborn etc.

In body parts it denote Heart, breast, eye balls, appendix, blood cells, awareness, pulses, lips etc.

In things/objects it denote Flower path, cooking skills, makeup artists, pottery industries, hotpot restaurant, barbecue restaurant, fast food restaurant, sole proprietor, lightnings, candle.

In plants/vegetations it denote Hemps, Chinese peony, rose, Japanese rose, Chinese cinnamon, mimosa (touch me not), pyrethrum, red beans etc.

In animals/living things it denote Firefly, cicada, earthworm, ladybird, hornet, scorpion, mosquito, fleas, grasshopper, viper, cockroach,

In Utensils/objects it denote the Microwave oven, induction cooker, fuel, power, lighting fixtures, toys, box/cases, lighters, battery, etc.

xix) Ding Chou Day Master 丁丑日元:

	Year	Month	Day Master	Hour
Heaven Stem			**Ding** 丁	
Earth Branch			**Chou** 丑	
Hidden Stem			己-EG 癸-SK 辛-IW	

This Day Pillar is termed "Midnight Cow Day 半月牛日".

This is an ominous Day Master. It has the harmful "Freak Error Calamities star" which denotes errors due to chance or random factors. It indicate the random factor why people can not get along well. (阴差阳错 yin cha yang cuo literary meant 'an accident arising from many causes'. This is a divination term coined by ancient masters to describe this type of calamities).

Chinese ancient saying: "".

When these calamities stars appeared at two or three pillar in the Month, Day or Hour pillars, the calamities is very serious.

However, if it only appear only in the Day Pillar, it is not so serious. The person will not have in-law family support. Even if the in-law is wealthy, it will be squander away. Over time it will cause enmity with in-law and separation.

People with this Stars are likely to have illegitimate children or siblings. Marriage are discussed during mourning and disagreements normally happen. Spouse cannot get along with parents. Cold wars within close kin. In work and career, they will let opportunities pass by and fail within sight of success.

Ding 丁 is like a candle fire (sacrificing (burning themselves out) to provide 'light'. They are very sensitive (waiver when there's a slight breeze). Ding Day Master folks like to burn mid-night oil (indicating they will be involved in night shift works).

Ding 丁 is Yin Fire, thus if there are too many other Yin Elements in the chart, this person is 'hypersensitive' and probably able to 'see' spirits and be able to communicate with them.

Folks with Ding Chou Day Master

丁丑日元 tends to be attracted to successful people. Better for them to settle down and establish a family. They need support and encouragement.

Ding Chou Day Master sat on its own 'wealth depository 财库'. So, whenever the Day Master energies are strengthened during the Current Year and/or 10 Year Cycle, this person will be rich. However, it is advised that such person marry late (after 28 years old).

Ding Chou Day is a very auspicious day for business opening celebration. Place a red color bull in the office to bring in the good business luck.

Ding Chou Day Master folks couple can venture into business together (as they will support each other).

Lady with Ding Chou Day Master, they will be very independent when young however they will be lonely after marriage. Their health will deteriorate after childbirth.

Guy with Ding Chou Day Master must choose a gal with good temper (to ensure a happy married life). However, not matter whom they choose it will not turn out to their ideal partner.

*** Folks with Ding Chou 丁丑日元 Day Master folks are likely to meet their future spouse born in the Year or Month of the Dragon, Horse, Goat, Dog 龙马羊狗年月 or when their spouse palace encountered clash, conflict or harm 夫妻宫被审型破害.

xx) Ding Mao Day Master 丁卯日元:

	Year	Month	Day Master	Hour
Heaven Stem			**Ding** 丁	
Earth Branch			**Mao** 卯	
Hidden Stem			乙 - IR	

This Day Pillar is termed "Night Rabbit Day 夜兔日".

Folks with this Day Master are intelligent and well educated. If this Day Master formed the Hai Mao Wei Three Combination 亥卯未三和局 or the Yin Mao Chen Three Meeting 寅卯辰三会局 this person is likely to be a successful and wealthy or attain a high-ranking position. But if their Day Master energies are 'weak' then they can only deputy or assistant.

Folks with Ding Mao Day Master 丁卯日元 sat on Indirect Resource star, thus are very adventurous and creative whom love the unexplained things such as UFO and high-tech. They have extraordinary abilities to 'see' through things very quickly.

When the Indirect Resource star shined at the Year Pillar it indicated this child is full of curiosity.

When the Indirect Resource star shined at the Month Pillar, it indicated this person curiosity is very high but lack the courage to explore.

When the Indirect Resource star shined during the Current Year or 10 Year Cycle, the Day Master will not be able to hold any cash, thus it is better to invest in properties, otherwise they will lose a lot of money, even bankruptcy.

Note: Indirect Resource star also indicated potential incurable illness. Folks with Indirect Resource stars need to approach financial issues with great care.

Ladies with this Day Master will bring good luck and wealth to her spouse after 43 years of age.

Guy with this Day Master, if they don't gamble, drink or womanize, after 40 year of year they will have a good and successful life.

No matter guy or gal, folks with this Day Master must have good repose/ understanding with spouse or financial matters.

*** Folks with Ding Mao 丁卯日元 Day Master are likely to meet their future spouse born in the Year or Month of the Tiger, Monkey, Pig 虎 猴 猪 年 月 or when their spouse palace encountered clash, conflict or harm 夫妻宫被审型破害.

xx.i) Ding Si Day Master 丁巳日元:

	Year	Month	Day Master	Hour
Heaven Stem			**Ding** 丁	
Earth Branch			**Si** 巳	
Hidden Stem			丙-RW 戊-HO 庚-DW	

This Day Pillar is termed " Night Snake Day 夜蛇日".

This Day Master is ominous as it is inflicted with the harmful "Lonely Phoenix Calamities star 孤鸾煞". If born in the Ding Si Hour this person will have short lifespan.

Folks with Ding Si Day Master 丁巳日元 will likely co-habitat but not get married. Si 巳 Fire have hidden stem of Rob Wealth star and Direct Wealth star. Rob Wealth star will suppress the Direct Wealth talents and skills.

Furthermore, this Rob Wealth star have Month Command, so this person must not venture into business with 'Friends' or peers as the business will surely go burst. Such people can only venture into business on their own (to ensure success).

Lady with this Day Master need to find someone whom can pamper, love and constantly encourage her.

Lady with this Day Master have a special ability to attract the attention of the opposite sex. However, unfortunately after marriage they will be influenced by the "Lonely Phoenix Calamities star 孤鸾煞" which when activated will cause wife and husband conflicts and quarrels, which resulted in multi-marriage, if not separated or divorced the other party will die first.

Lady with this Day Master easy get married due to the double fire energies (they can't control themselves once they meet someone, they 'like').

People with Hurting Officer stars 伤官星 in the hidden stem are likely to be scolded by spouse frequently. So guy with Hurting Officer star must be able to endure the wife scolding and nagging.

*** Folks with Ding Si 丁巳日元 Day Master are likely meet their future spouse born in the Year or Month of the Tiger, Monkey Pig 虎猴猪年月 or when their spouse palace encountered clash, conflict or harm 夫妻宫被审型破害.

xx.ii) Ding Wei Day Master 丁未日元:

	Year	Month	Day Master	Hour
Heaven Stem			**Ding 丁**	
Earth Branch			**Wei 未**	
Hidden Stem			己-EG 丁-Fr 乙-IR	

This Day Pillar is termed "Night Goat Day 夜羊日".

This is an ominous Day Master. It is inflicted with the harmful ""Freak Error Calamities star" which denotes errors due to chance or random factors. It indicate the random factor why people can not get along well. Thus marriage will not last.

Main hidden stem Yi 己 Earth is the Eating God star 食神星 indicating this person is pretty/handsome but like to eat too much thus is likely to be plumb. Lady are good housewife.

Folks with Ding Wei Day Master 丁未日元 are easily troubled by close kins problems and cause an happy marriage life. They are usually very concerned about their welfare.

Generally, wife of Ding Wei Day Master is rather plumb (this is due to the Eating God star 食神星 and Friend star 比肩星 in the spouse palace). However, the Friend star 比肩星 in the spouse palace also indicated a likelihood of separation or divorce.

Lady with this Day Master are easily win over (due to their sentimental nature). Besides they are not choosy type, as long as they have feeling for the guy, they will not hesitate to marry them.

Note: In a guy chart, whenever the spouse palace encounter conflict or clashes, their Peach Blossom stars will shines, indicating affections issues (detrimental to married family but are good for those in entertainment and/or networking as their contacts will increase).

In a lady chart whenever their spouse palace encountered conflict/clashes, they will not stay long with their partner (indicating likelihood of separation/divorce).

Ladies with this Day Master, during their pregnancy and/or child delivery period, they are extra-sensitive to occult phenomenon (likely to be able to 'see' spirits/ghosts).

*** Folks with Ding Wei 丁未日元 Day Master are likely meet their future spouse born in the Year or Month of the Rat, Cow, Dog 鼠 牛 狗 年 月 or when their spouse palace encountered clash, conflict or harm 夫妻宫被审型破害.

xx.iii) Ding You Day Master 丁酉日元:

	Year	Month	Day Master	Hour
Heaven Stem			**Ding** 丁	
Earth Branch			**You** 酉	
Hidden Stem			辛 - IW	

This Day Pillar is termed "Night Cockerel Day 夜鸡日".

This is an auspicious Day Master but spouse are too romantic (note: You 酉 is a Peach Blossom star).

The main hidden stem You 酉 an Indirect Wealth star also indicate this person is an night owl and love learning. This person is elegant and intelligent, loved and admired by all.

Folks with Ding You 丁酉日元 Day Master is known as Fire Phoenix 火凤凰 (You 酉 is a phoenix).

Guy with this Day Master have laborer life 劳怒命 (work and work whole life). They are mostly businessmen or self-employed entrepreneurs.

Folks with this Day Master, when the Earth palace are Fire energies domain, their spouse and/or children usually demised before them 克妻克子.

Lady with this Day Master better to find a husband with good financial standing to have a stable married life. They will do well if they venture into business.

Folks with this Day Master frequently have fatal stomach and intestines issues (You 酉 Metal melted by Ding 丁 Fire).

Folks with this Day Master must not gamble (surely loose money - Indirect Wealth star denote unstable income).

When the Earth energies are strong (especially when it shine at the Hour Pillar), even after marriage, these folks will reunites with ex-lover. (Earth produce Metal indicating reignite old 'frame').

*** Folks with Ding You 丁酉日元 Day Master are likely meet their future spouse born in the Year or Month of the Rat, Rabbit, Dog, Cockerel 鼠 兔 狗 鸡 年 月 or when their spouse palace encountered clash, conflict or harm 夫妻宫被审型破害.

xx.iv) Ding Hai Day Master 丁亥日元:

	Year	Month	Day Master	Hour
Heaven Stem			**Ding** 丁	
Earth Branch			**Hai** 亥	
Hidden Stem			壬-DA 甲-DR	

This Day Pillar is termed "Night Pig Day 夜猪日".

This is an auspicious Day Master but inflicted with the harmful "The 10 Abomination Defeat calamities star 十恶大败煞" that bring disappointments and disasters. "10 Abomination" （十恶） meant unpardonable serious crimes; "Defeat" （大败） meant nothing left (money, food etc) totally eliminated.

Ancient folks believed that those with this calamities star will not inherit ancestors wealth, status, nor business due to various offenses.

Lady with this Day Master are likely to marry a wealthy, upright and successful husband.

Folks with Ding Hai Day Master 丁亥日元 which sat on a Direct Resource star 正印星 (three or more) usually place their career in top priority. Usually they will take care of their family too.

Note: Those with too many (three or more) Direct Authority star正官星 in their chart usually don't believe in occult or metaphysics (so they don't believe in Bazi divination as well).

Most ladies with this Day Master love their husband and care for the family. They will bring luck and wealth to their husband.

Married couple with this Day Master are loving and respect each other (Note: Ding丁 Fire clashes Hai亥 Water whereas Hai亥 Water produced Jia甲 Wood at the hidden stem).

*** Folks with Ding Hai 丁亥日元 Day Master are likely meet their future spouse born in the Year or Month of the Tiger, Snake, Monkey, Pig 虎 蛇 猴 猪 年 月 or when their spouse palace encountered clash, conflict or harm 夫妻宫被审型破害.

Chapter 5 :
Wu Yang Earth 戊阳土:

Wu Yang Earth occupied the central region.

In astrology it represent the Saturn planet.

In older times, most dams are built with mud(earth), thus Wu Earth 'control' Ren Water.

When black cloud covers the sky 乌云遮天 : Wu Earth destroy/control Ren Water.

When black cloud covers the Day 乌云蔽日: Wu Earth diminishes Bing Fire.

When black cloud cover the star 乌云遮星: Wu Earth diminishes Ding fire.

Blowing wind disperse cloud 风吹云散: thus, Yi Wood destroy Wu Earth.

At Heaven Stem it represents black cloud, fog/mist 雾. In Bazi concept, Bing Fire is most afraid of Wu Earth (because it can block off the Bing's fire heat and light.)

At Earth hidden stem it represent justice, security such as wall and laws.

It also denotes mountain range, thus is known as Yang Earth, also classified as 'sunset earth 霞土'; it also denotes sweet taste, a male deep strong and firm voice. In body system it denotes stagnation. It represents things crude and boorish.

It also denotes part of the body where there is fresh such as face, stomach, chest, digestive system, buttock, internal organs etc.

In general, it denotes an honest and considerate disposition, foolish and mother earth, ores and minerals, porcelain, overhead beam, room, construction workers, finance, eco-farm, city wall, building corners, wall, bridge, meat, wealth, big border, stomach, growth, capital etc.

In land/properties it denotes Mountain ridge, vigilant, cornfield, open land/field, temple, monastery, warehouse, car park etc.

In people it denote Officer in charge, Benefactor 贵人, prison guard, customer, abattoir, fat person, ugly woman etc.

In emotions/feeling it denote Honesty, frank, stubborn, firm & resolute, conservative, independent etc.

In body parts it denotes Stomach, digestive system, eye bags, nose, teeth, back, joints, cholesterol etc.

xx.v) Wu Zi Day Master 戊子日元:

	Year	Month	Day Master	Hour
Heaven Stem			Wu 戊	
Earth Branch			Zi 子	
Hidden Stem			癸-DW	

This Day Pillar is termed "Earth Rat Day 土鼠日".

This is an auspicious Day Master of the "Star of the Six Elegant Day 六秀日" Star of the 'Six Elegant Day' are Stars of outstanding writings and surpassing splendid. Individual born on these Day are extremely intelligent, brilliant natural disposition, multi-talented, highly educated, great desire for knowledge, excellent reflect, a born artist, writer and publisher. They are usually introvert and frequently a loner.

Folks with Wu Zi Day Master 戊子日元, when the natal chart has strong 'Friends' 比肩星 and Rob Wealth stars 劫才星, their spouse will surely demise before them 克夫、克妻. Also indicate multiple marriage.

When the Eating God star 食神星入库 fall in the 'wealth depository' (i.e., appear at the auxiliary hidden stem), this person will live in poverty. (Eating God star 食神星 are the product of the Day Master, e.g., Earth produce Metal, therefore Metal is the Earth Element Eating God star 食神星; Water produce Wood; thus, Wood is Water Eating God star 食神星.) But if the Eating God star 食神星 is 'revealed' at the Heaven Stem, it indicated the time when you will not be poor.

When the Day Master sat on its Wealth star (like this Wu Zi Day Master), this person will never poor. (Note: When the Wealth stars are being conflicted or clashed, it indicates a loss of wealth such as job lost or separation from wife).

Folks with this Day Master (no matter male or female), they are usually well to do, have good parents and public relationships.

Sidetrack: To determine the health of close kins (based on children chart):

Eldest Child chart:

	Year	Month	Day	Hour
Heaven Stem	**Grandfather** palace	**Father** palace		
Heaven Branch	**Grandmother** palace	**Mother** palace **Younger** siblings		

Second Child chart:

	Year	Month	Day	Hour
Heaven Stem	**Father** palace	**Elder** Siblings		
Heaven Branch	**Mother** palace	**Younger** siblings		

Third Child chart:				
	Year	Month	Day	Hour
Heaven Stem	Father palace	2nd Sibling palace		
Heaven Branch	Mother palace	4th sibling palace		

Forth Child chart:				
	Year	Month	Day	Hour
Heaven Stem	Father palace	3rd sibling palace		
Heaven Branch	Mother palace	5th sibling palace		

In a male destiny, when the Direct Resource star 正印星 shined at the Heaven stem and also shined at the hidden stem 正印星有根, this person will have a stable life.

When the Direct Wealth star 正财星 shined at the hidden stem and also 'revealed' at the Heaven stem 正财星投出, this person will do well in business. However, when this star is 'revealed' also indicated the business will go burst, thus Wealth stars must not be 'revealed'.

Lady with this Day Master will either be single whole life or will have a good husband. They must not be impatient when finding a husband or else easily mismatched. If their future husband is recommended by friends or close kins, then her married life is likely to be blissful. They must not be stubborn or else difficult for her to find a suitable husband.

This Day Master sat on a strong Peach Blossom star, indicated to be alone such as cook or writer), i.e., they must utilize their public relationship abilities. successful they must be sociable and work in an environment with many people (not in self-centered job or position where they work

*** Folks with Wu Zi 戊子日元 Day Master are likely meet their future spouse born in the Year or Month of the Rabbit, Horse, Cockerel, Goat 兔 五 鸡 羊 年 月 or when their spouse palace encountered clash, conflict or harm 夫妻宫被审型破害.

xx.vi) Wu Yin Day Master戊寅日元:

	Year	Month	Day Master	Hour
Heaven Stem			**Wu** 戊	
Earth Branch			**Yin** 寅	
Hidden Stem			甲-SK 丙-IR 戊-Fr	

This Day Pillar is termed "Earth Tiger Day 土龙日".

Folks with this Wu Yin Day Master 戊寅日元 need to be very patient in all their undertakings, including finding a spouse. However, guy with this Day Master will slowing destroy their wife (Wood beneath Earth will slowly deteriorate).

They will always be impatient and strong headed due to the Seven Killing star

七杀星 and 'Friends' star 比肩星 at the spouse palace. These stars are indicating problematic married life, i.e., separation or divorce.

These folks will find it difficult to find job due to these two inauspicious stars (Seven Killing star 七杀星 and 'Friends' star 比肩星).

Folks with this Day Master born in Shen 申 Month or Shen 申 Hour, their married life is likely to be problematic (Shen 申 Metal clashed with Jia 甲 Wood).

Lady with this Day Master better to marry before 29 but not 30 years of age or after, otherwise their married life will not be blissful. Early marriage will bring good luck and wealth to husband.

Note: When the spouse palace has Indirect Resource star 偏印星, this person must avoid marrying an impatient and rashful person (those with Seven Killing or Friends star 七杀 比肩星) to have a peaceful married life.

When the spouse palace has 'Friends' 比肩星, this person is very impatient and rashful and also place friends more important than their close kins, resulting in unhappy family life, which will cause separation or divorce.

*** Folks with Wu Yin 戊寅日元 Day Master are likely meet their future spouse born in the Year or Month of the Snake, Monkey, Pig 巳 申 猪 年 月 or when their spouse palace encountered clash, conflict or harm 夫妻宫被审型破害.

xx.vii) Wu Chen Day Master
戊辰日元:

	Year	Month	Day Master	Hour
Heaven Stem			**Wu** 戊	
Earth Branch			**Chen** 辰	
Hidden Stem			戊-Fr 乙-DA 癸-DW	

This Day Pillar is termed "Earth Dragon Day 土龙日".

This is an auspicious Day Master (Day Stem 'rooted' thus the Day Master energies are strong). Hidden stem Wu Earth is also a Fire energy, which is a Resource star manifesting a 'Authority star Resource star mutually produce each other 官印相生' a very auspicious occurrence that bring wealth and frame.

In a male destiny with Wu Chen Day Master 戊辰日元 (as the spouse palace have 'Friends' star 比肩星 and Direct Wealth stars 正财星) wife must submit to him or else there will be quarrels and arguments resulting in an unhappy family life.

However, if the spouse palace have Direct Authority and Direct Wealth stars without the present of the 'Friends' star, this wife is very virtuous and faithful. She will take very good care of the household affairs. It is very unlikely they will be separated or divorce.

Note: The Direct Authority star at the spouse palace indicated this guy joy/career is stable. Direct Authority star is most auspicious when it shined at the Month pillar, indicating this person will hold high position with authority(power).

In a female destiny when there're 'Friends' and Direct Authority stars at the spouse palace, indicated she will submit to her husband. When her spouse palace have Direct Wealth star at the auxiliary hidden stem, it indicated she have high respect for her father.

Note: When the Direct Wealth star shined at the Year Heaven stem, it indicated relationship with father is very good.

When the Direct Resource star shined at the Year Branch, it indicated the relationship with the mother is very good. Its good to stay with parents.

However, if the Year Stem does not have Direct Wealth star and the Year Branch does not have the Direct Resource star, it indicated this person cannot live with their parent (as there will be frequent quarrels and arguments).

Whenever the 'Friends' star 比肩星 shined at the spouse main hidden stem, it is better to marry late (preferably after 28 years of age) to avoid multi-marriage problems.

There's an ancient saying: 男最忌夫妻不同命;

Female most like stove/kin facing 'extinct' destiny 女最喜炉灶向绝命。

Folks with this Day Master (Wu Chen 戊辰）they're likely to have a well to do life (as Chen辰 is Wu's wealth depository 财库).

*** Folks with Wu Chen 戊辰日元 Day Master are likely meet their future spouse born in the Year or Month of the Cow, Rabbit, Dragon, Dog 牛 兔 龙 狗 年 月 or when their spouse palace encountered clash, conflict or harm 夫妻宫被审型破害.

xx.viii) Wu Wu Day Master 戊午日元:

	Year	Month	Day Master	Hour
Heaven Stem			**Wu** 戊	
Earth Branch			**Wu** 午	
Hidden Stem			丁-DR 己-RW	

This Day Pillar is termed "Earth Cow Day 土牛日".

This is an ominous Day Master. It is inflicted with the harmful "Lonely Phoenix Calamities star 孤鸾煞" which when activated will cause wife and husband conflicts and quarrels, that resulted in multi-marriage, if not separated or divorced the other party will die first.

However, such person are very kind (Wu 戊 Earth at Heaven stem depended on Wu 午 Fire at Earth Branch to produce it). This also indicated that such person are easily manipulated by other.

Folks with Wu Wu Day Master 戊午日元 can suddenly become wealthy (when the right time comes).

Folks with this Wu Wu Day Master 戊午日元 when their 'useful gods 用神星' are Fire Element, they are likely to have a kind and virtuous wife.

If their 'harmful gods 忌神星' are Fire Elements, then their marriage will not last due to the hot tempers' personality clashes.

Note: This Day Master had a 'Rob Wealth star 劫才星' at the spouse palace hidden stem, indicated these people will not be able to detain their wealth/monies. It also indicated loss of job or separation or divorce.

Folks with this Day Master, when the Fire Elements are 'revealed' at the Heaven stem and the spouse have 'bone weight 骨重两' more than 4 taels 四两钱, the guy will surely be wealthy.

Folks with this Day Master, if their 'harmful god 忌神' is Earth Element, then they will easily become bankrupt or poor.

*** Folks with Wu Wu 戊午日元 Day Master are likely meet their future spouse born in the Year or Month of the Rat, Cow, Rabbit, Horse 鼠 牛 兔 马 年 月 or when their spouse palace encountered clash, conflict or harm 夫妻宫被审型破害.

xx.ix) Wu Shen Day Master 戊申日元:

	Year	Month	Day Master	Hour
Heaven Stem			**Wu** 戊	
Earth Branch			**Shen** 申	
Hidden Stem			庚-EG 壬-IW 戊-Fr	

This Day Pillar is termed "Earth Monkey Day 土猴日".

This is an ominous Day Master. It is inflicted with the harmful "Freak Error Calamities star 阴差阳错" as well as the harmful "'Lonely Phoenix Calamities star 孤鸾煞'.

"Freak Error Calamities star" denotes errors due to chance or random factors. It indicates the random factor why people cannot get along well. (阴差阳错 yin cha yang cuo literary meant 'an accident arising from many causes'. This is a divination term coined by ancient masters to describe this type of calamities).

When these calamities stars appeared at two or three pillar in the Month, Day or Hour pillars, the calamities is very serious.

However, if it only appears only in the Day Pillar, it is not so serious. The person will not have in-law family support. Even if the in-law is wealthy, it will be squander away. Over time it will cause enmity with in-law and separation.

People with this Stars are likely to have illegitimate children or siblings. Marriage are discussed during mourning and disagreements normally happen. Spouse cannot get along with parents. Cold wars within close kin. In work and career, they will let opportunities pass by and fail within sight of success.

"'Lonely Phoenix Calamities star 孤鸾煞" in which wife and husband can't get along, indicated multi-marriage, if not separated or divorced the other party will die first.

Note: This Day Master hidden stem Geng庚 its Eating God star 食神星 depended on the Wu戊 its 'Friends' star 比肩星 to be efficacious, indicated this person will neglect their family and placed priorities in their job/career. Furthermore, when their job/career is established, this person is likely to have extra-marital affairs 事业有成外面有人。

Thus, folks with Wu Shen Day Master 戊申日元 should marry late (preferably after 28 years of age as they should work to establish their job/career first).

In a lady destiny, this Wu Wu Day Master folks loved their daughter (due to the Eating God 食神星).

If there's a Hurting Officer star伤官星, then she will love the son more.

Note: Lady with Hurting Officer star伤官星 will always scold their husband.

Lady with this Day Master (Wu Shen) are too sensitive and suspicious. Their marriage life is problematic thus separation or divorce is very likely.

Folks with this Day Master (both male and female) are inflicted with the harmful "Lonely Phoenix Calamities star 孤鸾煞" which when activated will cause wife and husband conflicts and quarrels, that resulted in multi-marriage, if not separated or divorced the other party will die first.

Note: If t0he first born is a girl, this lady is likely to remarry.

If the first born is a son, this guy is likely to remarry.

*** Folks with Wu Shen 戊申日元 Day Master are likely meet their future spouse born in the Year or Month of the Tiger, Snake, Pig 虎 蛇 猪 年 月 or when their spouse palace encountered clash, conflict or harm 夫妻宫被审型破害.

xxx) Wu Xu Day Master戊戌日元:

	Year	Month	Day Master	Hour
Heaven Stem			**Wu** 戊	
Earth Branch			**Xu** 戌	
Hidden Stem			戊-Fr 辛-HO 丁-DR	

This Day Pillar is termed "Earth Dog Day 土狗日".

This Day Master is inflicted with the harmful "The 10 Abomination Defeat calamities star 十恶大败煞" which bring disappointments and disasters.

"10 Abomination" （十恶） meant unpardonable serious crimes;

"Defeat" （大败） meant nothing left (money, food etc) totally eliminated..

This Day Master is also a "Star of Dipper Noble (魁罡星Kui Gang star) which are part of the Big Dipper constellation that represent limits, things that is out of reach, always fluctuating.

Chart with a strong Day Master when encounter this Star, the individual can become a millionaire. However, when the Day Master is weak and was clashed, counter-control or encounter 'punishment', it can bring disaster or calamities.

When there is no favorable combinations, female marriage life will encounter problem.

Male will easily encounter disaster and calamities and can even be jailed.

However, if the individual is physically ill or poor, this Star can help advert disaster and calamities.

Folks with this Wu Xu Day Master 戊戌日元 are usually selfish, stubborn and annoying.

Furthermore, they have 'Kui Gang 魁罡" destiny in which whenever they encounter a Chou丑 year during the Current Year Cycle or 10 Year Cycle, their lifespan are threaten.

Folks with Wu Xu Day Master 戊戌日元 their wife will always scold him (this is due to the Hurting Officer star伤官星 at the spouse palace.

After marriage, their will encounter extra-marital problems. Thus, must avoid overseas assignments.

Lady with this Day Master faces difficult and pressurized married life (two Earth Element character will find it difficult to be together due to their strong ego). They frequently have children's problems such as educations, bad behaviors, unfilial etc.

Ladies are likely to develop dementia after childbirth. Thus, husband must understand this and be more loving and caring towards their wife after childbirth.

Folks with this Day Master are strongly influenced by their mother. They regard their mother as a most perfect person. Thus, Day Master wife must lead a respectful and upright life, setting good example for her children.

Folks with this Day Master should not marry too young, better to marry after 28 years of age otherwise the guy will cause the wife early death and lady will cause their husband early death 严重克夫型妻. They are also detrimental to mother too 克母.

Note : Folks with this Day Master, their children are likely to demise before them 此命格容易白发送黑发.

Note: Folks with 'Friend' star 比肩星 at the spouse hidden stem are likely to squander off ancestor inheritances.

*** Folks with Wu Wu 戊午日元 Day Master are likely meet their future spouse born in the Year or Month of the Rat, Cow, Rabbit, Horse 鼠 牛 兔 马 年 月 or when their spouse palace encountered clash, conflict or harm 夫妻宫被审型破害.

Chapter 6 :
Yi Yin Earth 已阴土：

Yin Earth also represent the central region.
Yi 已 is Yin Earth. The younger brother of Wu Earth.
At the Heaven stem it denote vital energies;
At the Earth hidden stem, it denote fertile (cultivable) earth.
Pure energies rose, merged with heaven energies then descended, producing all things, thus known as Yin Earth.

Yi已 Earth denote cloud in the sky. It also represent sweet taste, graceful music. In places: It denote crops field, cemetery, plateau, bedroom, delivery room, atrium etc.

In people: It denote housewife, wife, farmer, manual worker, typist, secretary, customer service etc.

In emotions: It denote kindness, honest, magnanimous, reserved, gentle, yielding, greedy, stingy etc.

In body parts: It denote the spleen, pancreas, muscle, esophagus, abdomen, eyes, stones, autism, undernourished etc.

In things/objects: It denote Military wagon, city plan, preschool, nurse, gynecologist, fermentation factory etc.

In plants/vegetation: It denote cotton, sesame, Chinese foxglove, Atractylodes, polygonatum plant, longan fruits, potato, autumn crops etc.

In animals: It denote cow, panda, bear, mule, bees, spider, fowl etc.

In utensils/accessories: It denote the four treasures of Study (brush, ink, paper, ink stone), underwear, sterilized cotton, napkin, toilet paper, shoe, belt, seasoning etc.

xxx.i) Yi Chou Day Master 乙丑日元:

	Year	Month	Day Master	Hour
Heaven Stem			**Yi** 乙	
Earth Branch			**Chou** 丑	
Hidden Stem			己-Fr 癸-IW 辛-EG	

This Day Pillar is termed "Land Cow Day 地牛日".

This is an auspicious Day Master. It is one of the "Star of the Six Elegant Day 六秀日" This star denotes outstanding writings and surpassing splendid. Individual born on these Day are extremely intelligent, brilliant natural disposition, multi-talented, highly educated, great desire for knowledge, excellent reflect, a born artist, writer and publisher. They are introvert and frequently a loner. Lady with this Day Master are manly.

Folks with Yi Chou Day Master 乙丑日元 are always in two minds (this is due to the Day Master main Element 'rooted' in the spouse palace).

Furthermore, they are unable to change their habits or thinking.

Note: Whenever there's a 'Friend' star 比肩星 shined at the spouse palace it indicated a likelihood of separation or divorce. Thus, better for these folks to marry late (preferably after 28 year of age).

In a male destiny, when there's a Eating God 食神星 at the spouse palace auxiliary stem, it indicated this person can save money. When this Eating God 食神星 is 'revealed' at the Heaven stem, this person will do well in doing business.

In a lady destiny, when there's an Indirect Wealth star shined at the Month hidden stem, they are not suitable to be housewife as they always thinking of doing business and making money, thus they will neglect their family.

*** Folks with Wu Yi Chou 已丑日元 Day Master are likely meet their future spouse born in the Year or Month of the Dragon, Horse, Goat, dog 龙 马 羊 狗 年 月 or when their spouse palace encountered clash, conflict or harm 夫妻宫被审型破害..

xxx.ii) Yi Mao Day Master 已卯日元:

	Year	Month	Day Master	Hour
Heaven Stem			**Yi** 已	
Earth Branch			**Mao** 卯	
Hidden Stem			乙 -SK	

This Day Pillar is termed "Land Rabbit Day 地兔日".

This Day Master is ominous. Main hidden stem is Seven Killing star an harmful star that denotes sickness and troubles.

If the Year Pillar is also Yi Mao 已卯, one of their ancestors are crippled.

If the Month Pillar is also Yi Mao 已卯, parent cannot get along.

Yi Mao 已卯 Day Pillar indicated this person will be critical ill during their youth.

If the Hour Pillar is also Yi Mao 已卯, indicate children are not filial and this person may not have a peaceful death.

Folks with this Yi Mao Day Master 已卯日元, in a lady destiny, when the Seven Killing star 七杀星 shined alone without the present of Authority stars 官星 and another Seven Killing star, this lady is very 'pure' in relationship and affections. They are unlikely to be involved in extra-marital affairs.

Note: When during the 10 Year Luck Cycle the 'first three consecutive Cycle '大运内三格', whenever there's a Seven Killing star, it indicated a turbulent period of disasters with many changes and up and down.

Male with Yi Mao Day Master 已卯日元 usually had problematic married life. They will find it hard to find a suitable partner. This is due to the Seven Killing star which is harmful to the Day Master.

Furthermore, if the Seven Killing star is a 'harmful god忌神' this guy will mistreat or bully his wife. Moreover, most wife of this Day Master will have very strong character, so its difficult to get along.

:

i) Male born in Yang Year 阳男 & Female born in Yin Year 阴女:

10 Heaven Stem 十天干									
1	2	3	4	5	6	7	8	9	10
甲	乙	丙	丁	戊	已	庚	辛	壬	癸

12 Earth Branch 十二地支											
1	2	3	4	5	6	7	8	9	10	11	12
子	丑	寅	卯	辰	巳	午	未	申	酉	戌	亥

An illustration: A A guy born in 2006 May 6th @1323 Hr

	Year	Month	Day	Hour
Heaven Stem	Bing 丙 3	Ren 壬 9	Ren 壬 9	Ding 丁 4
Earth Branch	Xu 戌 11	Chen 辰 5	Chen 辰 5	Wei 未 8

Starting from Year Stem Bing +3; Ren +9; Ren +9; Ding +4; total = 23 year old. So, this guy is likely to marry at age 23 otherwise he should marry at age 34 (23 + Xu 11). If he marry at 23 year old it is very auspicious as this is termed heaven destined date.

An illustration: A A gal born in 1987 May 3rd @1323 hr

	Year	Month	Day	Hour
Heaven Stem	Ding 丁 4	Jia 甲 1	Ren 壬 9	Ding 丁 4
Earth Branch	Mao 卯 4	Chen 辰 5	Zi 子 1	Wei 未 8

Starting from Year Stem Ding +4; Jia +1; Ren + 9; Ding +4; total = 18 year old. At 18 year old she may be too young to marry (still in school?), so we add Mao +4 = 22 year old. Now this is probably a ripe time to get marry.

ii) Male born in & Female born in :

10 Heaven Stem 十天干									
4	5	6	7	8	9	10	1	2	3
甲	乙	丙	丁	戊	已	庚	辛	壬	癸

12 Earth Branch 十二地支											
11	12	1	2	3	4	5	6	7	8	9	10
子	丑	寅	卯	辰	巳	午	未	申	酉	戌	亥

An example of a :

A guy born in 1951 August 22 @1155 Hr

	Year	Month	Day	Hour
Heaven Stem	Xin 辛 1	Bing 丙 6	Jia 甲 4	Geng 庚 10
Earth Branch	Mao 卯 2	Shen 申 7	Wu 午 5	Wu 午 5

Starting from Year Stem Xin +1; Bing +6; Jia +4; Geng +10 = total 21 years.

Yes, indeed this person (my friend) married at age 21-year-old.

An example of a :

A gal born in 1952 June 25 @ 0300 Hr

	Year	Month	Day	Hour
Heaven Stem	Ren 壬 2	Bing 丙 6	Ren 壬 2	Ren 壬 2
Earth Branch	Chen 辰 3	Wu 午 5	Yin 寅 1	Yin 寅 1

Starting from Year Stem Ren +2; Bing +6; Ren +2; Ren +2 = 12 year old, too young to marry, so we add Chen +3; Wu +5; Total 20 year old.

So, she is likely to marry at age 20 year old.

This method has a high degree of accuracy (proven by many cases).

Back to Yi Mao Day Master 已卯日元:

Generally, folks with this Day Master, guy will marry a beautiful wife while lady will marry to a handsome guy.

*** Folks with Yi Mao 乙卯日元 Day Master are likely meet their future spouse born in the Year or Month of the Tiger, Monkey, Pig 虎 猴 猪 年 月 or when their spouse palace encountered clash, conflict or harm 夫妻宫被审型破害..

xxx.iii) Yi Si Day Master 乙巳日元:

	Year	Month	Day Master	Hour
Heaven Stem			Yi 乙	
Earth Branch			Si 巳	
Hidden Stem			丙-DR 戊-RW 庚-HO	

This Day Pillar is termed "Land Snake Day 地蛇日".

This Day Master have the "Gold God star energies 金神星" which is an auspicious star that bring Wealth and honor.

When this Star in one's chart, it represent this person is resolute and have an upright character, intelligent, talented, very studious, are stubborn and have a strong destructive character.

Folks with Yi Si Day Master 乙巳日元, male doesn't care too much about his marriage. To him marriage is just a procedure. Such gal normally won't stay at home. He will spend most of this time away from home.

Furthermore, they are unlikely to have many friends. But he will not hesitate to lend a helping hand to friend in need (this is due to the Direct Resource star at the hidden stem).

Lady with this Day Master will spend all their time on children, especially on her son (because of Hurting Officer star at the hidden stem). They seldom have time for themselves nor her husband. This lady must also be well informed in general knowledge and current affairs (this is due to the Direct Resource star at the hidden stem).

Lady must be very careful when speaking to her husband, cannot be too blunt or direct as it will hurt her husband feelings (Hurting Officer star are very direct and it frequently don't care about the other party feeling. Thus, lady with Hurting Officer star will always scold their husband).

Male with this Day Master when they spend money, they need to consider the feeling of his wife (due to the Rob Wealth star劫才星 at the hidden stem.

*** Folks with Yi Si 乙巳日元 Day Master are likely meet their future spouse born in the Year or Month of the Tiger, Monkey Pig 虎 猴 猪 年 or when their spouse palace encountered clash, conflict or harm 夫妻宫被审型破害.

xxx.iv) Yi Wei Day Master 乙未日元:

	Year	Month	Day Master	Hour
Heaven Stem			**Yi** 乙	
Earth Branch			**Wei** 未	
Hidden Stem			己-Fr 丁-IR 乙-SK	

This Day Pillar is termed "Land Goat Day 地羊日".

This person love money but very petty. However, when their chart encountered the wealth stars during the Current Year and/or 10 Year Luck Cycle, they will suddenly become rich.

Folks with Yi Wei Day Master 已未日元, male is better to marry late to avoid separation (this is due to the 'Friend' star and Seven Killing star at the spouse palace hidden stem). Seven Killing star also indicated this person had uncontrolled hot temper.

They usually are unable to have the understanding of his wife.

They have no affinity with children (relationship usually very poor).

They are more closed to friends than close kins (this is due to present of the 'Friend' star).

Guy with 'Friend' and Indirect Resource stars in their spouse palace are usually more inclined to drinking and merry makings. This may lead to troubles.

Lady with this Day Master like to be independent and dislike the frequent companion of her husband.

Folks with this Day Master during the courtship need to understand each other characters and abilities. This is to ensure a cohesive married life.

They should not give up their occupation after marriage (for personal security reasons).

Before marriage, they should define their wealth and properties, that is yours and what is mind, should be agreed (to prevent legal issues when separated/divorce).

Note: Folks with this Day Master better to marry before 28-year-old, otherwise they are likely to demise young (this is due to the Indirect Resource star causing their weird thinking and behavior).

*** Note: Folks with this Day Master children are likely to demise before them "天火杀子". Yi Wei 已未 in Na Yin divination is termed Heavenly Fire 天火.

*** Folks with Yi Wei 乙未日元 Day Master are likely meet their future spouse born in the Year or Month of the Rat, Cow Dog 鼠 牛 狗 年 月 or when their spouse palace encountered clash, conflict or harm 夫妻宫被审型破害..

xxx.v) Yi You Day Master 乙酉日元:

	Year	Month	Day Master	Hour
Heaven Stem			**Yi** 乙	
Earth Branch			**You** 酉	
Hidden Stem			辛 - EG	

This is Day Pillar is termed "Land Cockerel Day 地鸡日".

This is a good Day Master as it have the "God of Literature star 文昌星" indicating this person love learning, intelligent and have good cultural abilities.

Folks with Yi You Day Master 乙酉日元 dislike other to interfere with their life, especially regarding relationships and marriage..

However, they don't hold any hateful and doesn't keep any unhappiness in their heart.

Male with this Day Master are very serious in all their undertakings, including relationship (this is due to the Eating God star 食神星.

This also make it difficult for him to find his ideal partner. However, these guys are usually good and caring husband.

Normally they prefer more matured or more knowledgeable lady.

Lady with this Day Master are advised not to give birth too many children (Eating God are produced from Day Master, thus it diminished the Day Master energies.

*** Folks with Yi You 巳酉日元 Day Master are likely to meet their future spouse born in the Year or Month of the Rat, Rabbit, Dog or Cockerel 子 卯 狗 鸡 年 月 (note: Rat Rabbit and Cockerel are Peach Blossom stars) or when their spouse palace encountered clash, conflict or harm 夫妻宫被审型破害.

xxx.vi) Yi You Day Master 巳酉日元:

	Year	Month	Day Master	Hour
Heaven Stem			Yi 己	
Earth Branch			Hai 亥	
Hidden Stem			壬-DA 甲-DW	

This Day Pillar is termed "Land Pig Day 地猪日".

This is an auspicious Day Master. Spouse are likely to have longevity. Hidden stem Direct Authority and Direct Wealth stars indicated this person are elegant, upright and wealthy.

Lady with this Day Master are likely to marry a good and caring husband.

This Yi Hai Day Master 己亥日元 is a very auspicious Day Master. Lady are usually virtuous wife. Guy will take their marriage very seriously (thus unlikely to be involved in extra-marital affairs).

This Day Master usually bring blessings.

Folks with this Day Master are usually very upright and law-abiding people. Normally they will settle down before building their career/business.

Lady marries during their 'heavenly destiny date' (see chapter xx.xi) Yi Mao Day Master 已卯日元 above) will have blissful married life. Their first born are usually a son (this will bring luck and success to her husband).

Folks with this Day Master are usually very loving and happy couple (but their chart must not have Yin寅 Si巳 Shen申 Hai亥. These stars will clash off the good blessings).

These folks are usually very tolerant of their partner shortcomings.

Folks with this Day Master will be most benefiting its auspicious energies if they have at least 4 taels 2 mael bone weight 四两二钱骨.

*** Folks with Yi Hai 已亥日元 Day Master are likely to meet their future spouse born in the Year or Month of the Tiger, Snake, Monkey, Pig 虎 蛇 猴 猪 年 月 or when their spouse palace encountered clash, conflict or harm 夫妻宫被审型破害.

Chapter 7 :
Geng Yang Metal 庚阳金

Geng Yang Metal represent the West. It denotes the universal austere power and authority.

In astrology it's the Mercury planet.

It denotes military weapons and warfare.

At Heaven stem it's a celestial unfeeling ice. It also it represents the Moon (due to its reflective properties).

At Earth Branch hidden stem it's a threatening cold (merciless) metal or weapon. Thus, it's a Yang Metal.

In Geography it denotes tide, passageway, passage, high-speed railroad, temple, shrine, lake/reservoir etc.

In people it denotes soldier, grandparents, formidable opponent, examinant etc.

In emotions/feeling it denotes firm/unyielding, courageous, killing/murder, unforgiving, vulgar, violent etc.

In body parts it denotes the large intestines, navel, bones, women's period, thyroid glands, menopause, fracture/ dislocation of joints, etc.

In things/objects it denotes inspection, transform, ailment, dead/injured, traffic accident, military affairs, car business, mining industry, lumbering, fugitive/flee from danger etc.

In plant/vegetation it denotes onion, garlic, Chinese chives, chrysanthemum, curry, radish, celery etc.

In animals it denotes tiger, leopard, lion, crocodile, termite, grasshopper, beetle, apes/monkey, cricket, woodpecker etc.

In utensils it denotes sword/knife, clock, drum, axe, arrow, saw, feathered products, automobiles, exercise equipment etc.

xxx.vii) Geng Zi Day Master
庚子日元:

	Year	Month	Day Master	Hour
Heaven Stem			**Geng** 庚	
Earth Branch			**Zi** 子	
Hidden Stem			癸-HO	

This Day Pillar is termed "Golden Rat Day 金鼠日".

This is an ominous Day Master. Main hidden stem Gui癸 the Hurting Officer star 伤官星 indicated wife are detrimental to husband女命克夫. Besides, she will always scold her husband, thus her married life is problematic.

Heaven Stem produces Earth Branch indicated this person is elegant and intelligent. But they are too frank and straight-forward. They are more loyal to friends.

These folks are suitable to be in the public security authority's department.

Folks with Geng Zi Day Master 庚子日元 have very strong ego, stubborn, cold and unbending personality.

These folks have very good business acumen thus will get wealthy easily. But they can't do by themselves, need to employ people to run the business and just oversea its operations.

They must place priority on family to have a peaceful family life.

Male with this Day Master their wife usually has poor health.

Normally they will stay single due to their high expectations and demands. They will decide and make all decisions of their marriage. They dislike wife to control them.

They must not marry within the first three 10 Year Cycle 內三年, in short marry late (preferably after 28-year-old) otherwise their married life will be problematic. Furthermore, they are unlikely to have son. Even if their wife can conceive, the likelihood of miscarriage is high.

Note: During the transition period when the Earth Branch changed over to the next Heaven Stem (地支跃天), this is a very crucial period when dramatic events happen (such as divorce, miscarriage, sudden death or company go burst).

Note: When the Eating God star are 'revealed' at the Heaven stem, especially during the Current Year Cycle, it indicates a prosperous period when a person will attain great success and wealth.

Lady with this Day Master will likely miss a marriage opportunity during her courtship time.

Note: Lady with Hurting Officer star 伤官星 will always scolds/bully her husband.

*** Folks with Geng Zi 庚子日元 Day Master are likely to meet their future spouse born in the Year or Month of the Rabbit, Horse, Cockerel, Goat 兔 马 鸡 羊 年 月 (note: Rabbit and Cockerel are Peach Blossom stars) or when their spouse palace encountered clash, conflict or harm 夫妻宫被审型破害.

xxx.viii) Geng Yin Day Master
庚寅日元:

	Year	Month	Day Master	Hour
Heaven Stem			**Geng** 庚	
Earth Branch			**Yin** 寅	
Hidden Stem			甲-IW 丙-SK 戊-IR	

This Day Pillar is termed "Golden Tiger Day 金虎日".

This Day Master is inflicted with the harmful "Freak Error Calamities star" denotes errors due to chance or random factors. It indicates the random factor why people cannot get along well. (阴差阳错 yin cha yang cuo literary meant 'an accident arising from many causes'). This is a divination term coined by ancient masters to describe this type of calamities).

When these calamities stars appeared at two or three pillar in the Month, Day or Hour pillars, the calamities is very serious.

However, if it only appears only in the Day Pillar, it is not so serious. The person will not have in-law family support. Even if the in-law is wealthy, it will be squander away. Over time it will cause enmity with in-law and separation.

People with this Stars are likely to have illegitimate children or siblings. Marriage are discussed during mourning and disagreements normally happen. Spouse cannot get along with parents. Cold wars within close kin. In work and career, they will let opportunities pass by and fail within sight of success.

Folks with this Geng Yin Day Master 庚寅日元 are likely to spent a lot of their time in their career/business (due to the Indirect Wealth star 偏才星).

Folks with Indirect Resource star have full of unique thinking and weird way of doing things. Example, they will surprise you with unexpected arrangement for your birthday. They will go all out to 'steal' someone girlfriend just for the thrill and excitement. Folks with Seven Killing star indicated they will not see eye to eye with their partner. It also indicated sickness. In the above example Seven Killing star is Bing Fire, indicated illness of the eyes and blood issues such as high blood. They should avoid womanizing as it will cause them to lose their wealth. They will get involved in affairs that later resulted in legal issues.

Ladies with Seven Killing star at the spouse palace and when this star also shined at the other three pillars, it indicated this lady will likely to be taken advantage by other guys (one night stand or after going to bed the guy will disappear overnight) or they will be cheated financially.

Folks with this Day Master need to be approach from their point of view, otherwise a dispute will surely happen (Geng Metal and Yin Wood clashed). Folks with this Day Master will do well if they change job/business during their matured years (Geng Metal destroyed Yin Wood). Especially during the third 10 Year Cycle pillar, example:

10 Gods	Current 2015 35 y/o	10 Year 2012-2021 32 yo	Year	Month	Day	Hour
	Indirect Resource	Hurting Officer	Direct Wealth	Direct Resource	Day Master (M)	Hurting Officer
Heaven Stem	Yi Wood	Wu Earth	Geng Metal	Jia Wood	Ding Fire	Wu Earth
Earth Branch	Wei Earth	Zi Water	Shen Metal	Shen Metal	Chou Earth	Shen Metal
Hidden Stem	Ji-EG Ding-Fr Yi-IR	Gui-SK	Geng-DW Ren-DA Wu-HO	Geng-DW Ren-DA Wu-HO	Yi-EG Gui-SK Xin-IW	Geng-DW Ren-DA Wu-HO
10 Year Cycle	2yo 1982 乙 2-6 酉 7-11	12yo 1992 丙 12-16 戌 17-21	22yo 2002 丁 22-26 亥 27-32	32yo 2012 戊 32-36 子 37-41	42yo 2022 己 42-46 丑 47-51	52yo 2032 庚 52-56 寅 57-61	62yo 2042 辛 62-66 卯 67-71	72yo 2052 壬 72-76 辰 77-81	82yo 2062 癸 82-86 巳 87-91	92yo 2072 甲 92-105 午 106!

The third 10 Year Cycle is Ding Hai age 22 to 32. During this period if they change job/career there will be many benefactors 贵人 coming to help/assist in all their endeavors.

*** Folks with Geng Yin 庚寅日元 Day Master are likely to meet their future spouse born in the Year or Month of the Snake, Monkey, Pig 蛇 猴 猪 年 月 or when their spouse palace encountered clash, conflict or harm 夫妻宫被审型破害..

xxx.ix) Geng Chen Day Master
庚辰日元:

	Year	Month	Day Master	Hour
Heaven Stem			**Geng** 庚	
Earth Branch			**Chen** 辰	
Hidden Stem			戊-IR 乙-DW 癸-HO	

This Day Pillar is termed "Golden Dragon Day 金龙日".

This is an auspicious Day Master. It has the "Star of Dipper Noble star 魁罡贵人星". This star represents limits, things that is out of reach, always fluctuating. Chart with a strong Day Master when encounter this Star, the individual can become a millionaire.

However, when the Day Master is weak and was clashed, counter-control or encounter 'punishment', it can bring disaster or calamities.

When there is no favorable combinations, female marriage life will encounter problem; Male will easily encounter disaster and calamities and can even be jailed.

However, if the individual is physically ill or poor, this Star can help advert disaster and calamities.

Folks with this Geng Chen Day Master庚辰日元, male are firm and good looking, female are pretty and charming.

However, they have 'Kui Gang魁罡" destiny in which whenever they encounter a Chou丑 year during the Current Year Cycle or 10 Year Cycle, their lifespan is threaten (see above example chart above. The fifth 10 Year Cycle pillar is Yi Chou (where Chou is age 42 to 46 years old, so this person have a very crucial period when their life is threaten, there will be a very serious disaster).

Folks with this Kui Gang destiny usually don't believe in the supernatural, thus usually they are 'free thinker'.

Males are likely to be successful businessmen, but their health are very bad. They are also very romantic and easily fall for lady charms.

Females are likely to live alone during old age. Mostly their marriage will fail.

If her first born is a son, then it is very likely she will remarry (not necessary divorce but could be due to her husband early demise).

If she had a daughter, then this child will not have long life.

When the Direct Wealth star are 'revealed' 正官透柱, it indicated a period of great wealth and prosperity. In the above chart Direct Wealth star Yi 乙 is 'revealed' at age 63 Yi Chou pillar 乙丑柱, thus this person is likely to become very wealthy at age 63 range (pity this person already old thus will not be able to enjoy the wealth).

It also indicated the age of demise.

This Day Master had many '"combinations":

i) Geng Metal combined with hidden stem Yi Wood to transform into a Metal energies.

ii) Hidden stem Wu Earth combined with hidden stem Gui Water to transform into a Water energies (there may be more depending on the other pillars stars).

'Combinations' indicated external/secret affairs, thus detrimental to marriage life.

*** Folks with Geng Chen 庚辰日元 Day Master are likely to meet their future spouse born in the Year or Month of the Cow, Rabbit, Dragon,

Dog 牛 兔 龙 狗 年 月 or when their spouse palace encountered clash, conflict or harm 夫妻宫被审型破害.

XL) Geng Wu Day Master 庚午日元:

	Year	Month	Day Master	Hour
Heaven Stem			**Geng** 庚	
Earth Branch			**Wu** 午	
Hidden Stem			丁-DA 己-DR	
10 Luck Cycle	3 yo 辛 未	13 yo 庚 午	23 yo 己 巳	33 yo 戊 辰	43 yo 丁 卯	53 yo 丙 寅	63 yo 乙 丑	73 yo 甲 子	83 yo 癸 亥

This Day Pillar is termed "Golden Horse Day 金马日".

This is a good Day Master. Spouse are usually pretty and attractive. Main hidden stem of Direct Authority and Direct Resource star indicated this person are likely to be an upright high ranking official. Note: The Heaven Stem and Branch conflicted, indicating a turbulent up and down of fortune.

This is a very auspicious Day Master for a lady as it indicated that she will marry a righteous and upright husband, especially when the its an 'useful god 喜用神', spouse palace sat on Direct Authority star, her husband star.

Mostly, they will have a good life.

Note: Direct Authority star in a male destiny denote power and authority. Direct Authority star in a female destiny denote stability.

Note: When the Direct Resource star is an 'useful god 喜用神', it indicated this person will likely be successful and attain frame and reputations.

Note: Interesting, when the spouse palace encounter clashes, it indicates your marriage period when you will meet your future spouse. However, when this clash happened it also indicated you will lose your job or business failed (when Direct Wealth star are clashed away).

When Day Master Geng Metal is suppressed by hidden stem Ding Fire, it denotes a 'hurt feeling' 心难收, indicating the husband will be mistreated by his wife, thus his feeling was 'hurt'.

When the hidden stem Yi Earth 巳土 produced the Geng Metal, happiness till old age 乐白头, as the wife will support and encourage her husband in all endeavors. Furthermore, it indicated this guy have good health.

In a lady destiny, it denoted she will always be loving and support her husband thus able to live a blissful life with her husband till old age.

*** Folks with Geng Wu 庚午日元 Day Master are likely to meet their future spouse born in the Year or Month of the Rat, Cow, Rabbit, Horse 鼠 牛 兔 马 年 月 or when their spouse palace encountered clash, conflict or harm 夫妻宫被审型破害.

XL.i) Geng Shen Day Master
庚申日元:

	Year	Month	Day Master	Hour
Heaven Stem			**Geng** 庚	
Earth Branch			**Shen** 申	
Hidden Stem			庚-Fr 壬-EG 戊-IR	
10 Luck Cycle	3 yo 辛未	13 yo 庚午	23 yo 己巳	33 yo 戊辰	43 yo 丁卯	53 yo 丙寅	63 yo 乙丑	73 yo 甲子	83 yo 癸亥

This Day Pillar is termed "Golden Monkey Day 金猴日".

This a good Day Master. It indicated a strong, healthy and wealthy person. However married life is problematic (due to the present of the 'Friend' star).

Lady with this Day Master are intelligent, elegance and attractive and will surely have a filial and successful children.

Folks with this Geng Shen Day Master 庚申日元 usually demand their spouse to have respect and obedient ('Friend' star at the main spouse hidden stem). They always felt their partner are not so suitable.

Folks with this Day Master are likely to suffer bloody disaster (spouse hidden stem Ren 壬 Water suppressed by Wu 戊 Earth) thus lady is likely to suffer miscarriage. They have to be very careful if conceived.

Note: When there's a Indirect Resource star 偏印星 (Indirect Resource star in Chinese is termed "xiao 梟", "xiao 梟" is a vulture like bird that ate its mother when they matured, this indicated that this person will likely do dramatic actions (frequently fatal) especially when their chart clashed the Year Deity 犯太岁年.

　　　　Lady with this Day Master usually have unhappy and problematic married life due to their strong character and ego ('Friend' star). They normally have sixth sense of coming events (due to the Indirect Resource star).
　　　　Guy with this Day Master better to marry late (after 28 year of age), due to their strong character and ego ('Friend' star), they are more closed to friends than close kins, thus their married life is usually problematic (separation/divorce rate is very high).

　　　　*** Folks with Geng Shen 庚申日元 Day Master are likely to meet their future spouse born in the Year or Month of the Tiger, Snake, Pig 虎 蛇 猪 年 月 or when their spouse palace encountered clash, conflict or harm 夫妻宫被审型破害.

XL.ii) Geng Xu Day Master
庚戌日元:

	Year	Month	Day Master	Hour
Heaven Stem			**Geng** 庚	
Earth Branch			**Xu** 戌	
Hidden Stem			戊-IR 辛-RW 丁-DA	
10 Luck Cycle	3 yo 辛未	13 yo 庚午	23 yo 己巳	33 yo 戊辰	43 yo 丁卯	53 yo 丙寅	63 yo 乙丑	73 yo 甲子	83 yo 癸亥

This Day Pillar is termed "Golden Dog Day 金狗日".

This Day Master sat on its own 'wealth depository财库 and with a strong Day Master energy, will surely be wealthy. They also process good literary skill, loyal to friends.

This Day Master have the auspicious "Star of Dipper Noble star 魁罡贵人星". This star represents limits, things that is out of reach, always fluctuating.

However, when the Day Master is weak and was clashed, counter-control or encounter 'punishment', it can bring disaster or calamities.

When there are no favorable combinations, female marriage life will encounter problem.

Male will easily encounter disaster and calamities and can even be jailed.

However, if the individual is physically ill or poor, this Star can help advert disaster and calamities.

Chart with this Geng Xu Day Master 庚戌日元, the main hidden stem 在本气 Indirect Resource star 偏印星 generally indicated their spouse have very poor health (note: besides Seven Killing star, Indirect Resource star also denote sickness).

The chance of suffer a stroke is very high, especially is there are more than 3 Indirect Resource star in the natal chart. Most stroke patient have Indirect Resource star in their chart.

Besides, folks with this Day Master usually end up with an unsuitable partner.

Note: When there's a Rob Wealth star 劫才星 at the secondary hidden stem 在中气 it indicated this person are unable to save money or retain wealth 不能守才. Thus, when Rob Wealth star appear during the Current Year Cycle, it indicated a year of financial difficulties (include lost of job or business failures).

Lady with Rob Wealth star at the secondary hidden stem在中气 will face danger if they have operations during their matured year.

Note: When the auxiliary stem 余气 had Direct Authority star 正官星 it indicated this person is penny wise pound foolish. These people are easily manipulated and being used.

Lady with this Day Master are usually caught between her family and in-law disputes.

However, if the Indirect Resource star shined at the Hour Pillar, it indicated this person will have filial children and will enjoy their care and loving.

*** Folks with Geng Xu Day Master庚戌日元 are likely to meet their future spouse born in the Year or Month of the Cow, Dragon, Goat, Cockerel 牛 龙 羊 鸡 年 月 or when their spouse palace encountered clash, conflict or harm 夫妻宫被审型破害.

Chapter 8 :
Xin Yin Metal 辛阴金

Xin Yin Metal 辛阴金, 五金之首, the chief of the Five Metal, the head of the Eight precious stone 八石的第一位, thus is termed the 'Firm Metal 刚金' aka 'Supple Metal 柔金'. It denotes the Autumn frost. It flourishes in lunar 8th month 酉月 when the dew condenses as frost, weather cleared, plants and vegetation withered yellow, thus Xin Yin Metal 辛阴金 have a harsh and destructive element.

In astrology, it is the purple energies 紫炁, hailstone.

At Heaven stem, it represents freezing frost.

At Earth Branch hidden stem it represents the 24 solar terms, the Cold Dew and Frost Descends 寒露和霜降

In places, it denotes silverware store, deity altar, mill, brothel, peninsula.

In people, it denotes a representative, court judge, lawyer, policewoman, maiden, spirit medium, prostitute, transsexual, a clown, in-laws etc.

In nature/temperament, it denotes grim, resolute, soft appearance but firm within, gentle and pure etc.

In body parts, it denotes lungs, teeth, throat, femur, thoracic cavity, metabolism, cuts, injuries, deformity etc.

In things/objects, it denotes innovation, exploit, divination, agency, women matter, acupuncture, moxibustion, surgery etc.

In plant/vegetation, it denotes bulb of fritillary, gastralia elata, wheat, scallion, garlic, leek, ginkgo etc. In animals, it denotes eagle, hound, centipede, gecko, antelope, rhinoceros, white tiger, cuckoo etc.

In utensils it denotes jewelries, ring, small bell, keys, hardware implements, needles, medicine pestle, ivory commodity, plaster cast, leather goods etc.

XL.iii) Xin Chou Day Master
辛丑日元:

	Year	Month	Day Master	Hour
Heaven Stem			**Xin** 辛	
Earth Branch			**Chou** 丑	
Hidden Stem			己-IR 癸-EG 辛-Fr	
10 Luck Cycle	3 yo 辛未	13 yo 庚午	23 yo 己巳	33 yo 戊辰	43 yo 丁卯	53 yo 丙寅	63 yo 乙丑	73 yo 甲子	83 yo 癸亥

This Day Pillar is termed "Glittering Cow Day 金光牛日".

Folks with this Day Master, guy is very handsome, lady have good physique, elegant and care for family.

Folks with this Xin Chou Day Master辛丑日元 will never apologies even they knew they are in the wrong. This is due to the Indirect Resource star at the spouse palace main hidden stem 日支本气. Note: Their parents took their marriage very seriously.

When there's a Eating God star 食神星 at the secondary hidden stem 在中气, this person is likely to have insomnia. It also indicated this person health is not good.

When the Day Master Element is 'rooted', their partner does not share their problems (always kept to themselves).

Folks with this Day Master can hardly be successful in business venture because: Yi己 Earth suppressed Gui癸 the wealth source and at the same time Gui癸 depended on Xin辛 Metal to produce it, thus Gui癸 energies are very very weak.

Lady with this Day Master will bring blissfulness to her the family. However, if their Eating God star are being suppressed or clashed, it indicated she will find it difficult to have a daughter. Also indicated their problems are self-imposed.

*** Folks with Xin Chou 辛丑日元 Day Master are likely to meet their future spouse born in the Year or Month of the Dragon, Goat, Dog 龙 马 羊 狗 年 or when their spouse palace encountered clash, conflict or harm 夫妻宫被审型破害.

XL.iv) Xin Chou Day Master 辛丑日元:

	Year	Month	Day Master	Hour
Heaven Stem			**Xin** 辛	
Earth Branch			**Mao** 卯	
Hidden Stem			乙 - IW	
10 Luck Cycle	3 yo 辛未	13 yo 庚午	23 yo 己巳	33 yo 戊辰	43 yo 丁卯	53 yo 丙寅	63 yo 乙丑	73 yo 甲子	83 yo 癸亥	

This Day Pillar is termed " Glittering Rabbit Day 金光兔日".

This Day Master is ominous as it has the harmful "Freak Error Calamities star" which denotes errors due to chance or random factors. It indicates the random factor why people cannot get along well. Thus, marriage will not last.

Furthermore, the spouse palace is a Peach Blossom star, indicating guy are too romantic and flirtatious.

Lady is pretty thus difficult to avoid guy attention. Besides being pretty they are also very romantic thus difficult to avoid Peach Blossom calamities and disasters.

Folks with this Xin Mao Day Master 辛卯日元 male need to understand his spouse point of view to have a happy family life. (Note: Xin辛 Metal suppress/clash Mao卯Wood).

If a male chart has no Direct Wealth star (his wife star), Indirect Wealth star will also represent his wife star.

However, if there is a Direct Wealth star and also have an Indirect Wealth star, this Indirect Wealth star will denote his 'lover'.

If the Day Master energies are strong, guy will have an virtuous wife.

Lady with this Day Master, after married there will be a lot of disagreements/ disputes with her husband (Indirect Wealth star denote she's not suitable for her husband). However, she will have control of the family affairs.

After married, it is better for her to go out and work instead of staying at home as a housewife.

In fact, if they venture out to work, they will have a lot of 'benefactors 贵人' coming to their aids.

Note: During the Current Year or 10 Year Cycle, when the Heaven Stem are clashed/suppressed by the Earth Branch, it indicated a coming disaster. Referring to above chart, at age 13, the Wu午 Fire Earth Branch clashed the Heaven stem Geng庚 Metal, indicated a period of fatal disaster.

Folks with this Day Master, after married they will easily be inflicted with the Peach Blossom star calamities, indicating extra-marital affairs, thus causing family problems (note: the spouse star Mao卯 is a Peach Blossom star).

*** Folks with Xin Mao辛卯日元 Day Master are likely to meet their future spouse born in the Year or Month of the Tiger, Monkey, Pig 虎 猴 猪 年 月 or when their spouse palace encountered clash, conflict or harm 夫妻宫被审型破害.

XL.v) Xin Si Day Master 辛巳日元:

	Year	Month	Day Master	Hour
Heaven Stem			**Xin** 辛	
Earth Branch			**Si** 巳	
Hidden Stem			丙-DA 戊-DR 庚-RW	
10 Luck Cycle	3 yo 辛未	13 yo 庚午	23 yo 己巳	33 yo 戊辰	43 yo 丁卯	53 yo 丙寅	63 yo 乙丑	73 yo 甲子	83 yo 癸亥

This Day Pillar is termed "Glittering Snake Day光蛇日".

This Day Master have the harmful "The 10 Abomination Defeat 十恶大败" that is a very ominous star that bring disappointments and disasters. "10 Abomination" (十恶) meant unpardonable serious crimes; "Defeat" (大败) meant nothing left (money, food etc.) totally eliminated.

The hidden stem Wu 戊 Earth reinforced the energies of the weak Day Master and further assisted by the Rob Wealth star, turned the 'weak' Day Master strong, thus this person will likely attain a high position authority position but unable to be wealthy (due to the Rob Wealth star present).

Folks with this Xin Si Day Master 辛巳日元 are likely to have a daughter then marry. OR

Will marry other people wife. This is due to the Seven Killing and Direct Resource star at the spouse palace (杀印在夫妻宫). Thus, it is advised not to go match making during this period, else they will marry someone's wife.

Male with this Day Master, his wife health is very bad (frequently fall sick). Note: Lady with this Day Master (as its main hidden stem is a Seven Killing star and the auxiliary star is a Rob Wealth star), the husband is likely to demise before her (indicating she will live her old age alone).

However, they usually have loving and caring husband.

She is likely to have unstable mentality due to the Seven Killing star and Direct Resource star creating a split personality.

However, if the Seven Killing star is a 'harmful god 忌神星 she will likely be a widow during her old age.

She should not marry early as it is detrimental to her husband (causing his early demise 克夫).

Note: When the secondary hidden stem is a Direct Resource star it indicated high education, thus the couple education standard must be more or less the same otherwise problem will arise where the one with higher education will look down on the other.

Folks with this Day Master are unlikely to have a son, or their son have short live (main hidden stem Seven Killing star effects).

*** Folks with Xin Si Day Master

辛巳日元 are likely to meet their future spouse born in the Year or Month of the Tiger, Monkey, Pig 虎 猴 猪 年 月 or when their spouse palace encountered clash, conflict or harm 夫妻宫被审型破害.

XL.vi) Xin Wei Day Master
辛未日元:

	Year	Month	Day Master	Hour
Heaven Stem			**Xin** 辛	
Earth Branch			**Wei** 未	
Hidden Stem			己-DR 丁-SK 乙-IW	
10 Luck Cycle	3 yo 辛未	13 yo 庚午	23 yo 己巳	33 yo 戊辰	43 yo 丁卯	53 yo 丙寅	63 yo 乙丑	73 yo 甲子	83 yo 癸亥

This Day Pillar is termed the "Glittering Goat Day 金光辛日".

This Day Master sat on its own 'wealth depository 财库 and with a strong Day Master energies (hidden stem Yi 己 its Direct Resource star strengthen the Day Master Xin 辛) thus this person will likely become wealth.

Lady is very romantic but will seize household power and control from hubby.

Folks with this Xin Wei Day Master 辛未日元 are perfectionist. They will keep their house sparkling clean (due to the Direct Resource star at the main hidden stem).

At the wedding day, the bride must be escorted out of her house under a red umbrella to ensure having good children and happy life till old age.

(Note: The couple new bed must not be touched by person born in the year of the Tiger. Very ominous.)

Male with this Day Master are easily influenced by other views. Female are very romantic and will be faithful to her husband.

The secondary hidden stem Steven Killing stars indicated this person will be rebellious during middle age and also very sickly (in the above case, the Seven Killing star is Ding Fire, indicated heart and blood issues). It also indicated this person will go wayward.

*** Folks with Xin Wei 辛未日元 Day Master are likely to meet their future spouse born in the Year or Month of the Rat, Cow, Dog 鼠 牛 狗 年 月 or when their spouse palace encountered clash, conflict or harm 夫妻宫被审型破害.

XL.vii) Xin You Master
辛酉日元:

	Year	Month	Day Master	Hour
Heaven Stem			**Xin** 辛	
Earth Branch			**You** 酉	
Hidden Stem			辛 - Fr	
10 Luck Cycle	3 yo 辛未	13 yo 庚午	23 yo 己巳	33 yo 戊辰	43 yo 丁卯	53 yo 丙寅	63 yo 乙丑	73 yo 甲子	83 yo 癸亥

This Day Pillar is termed "Glittering Cockerel Day 金光鸡日".

This Day Master have the harmful "Freak Error Calamities star" which denotes errors due to chance or random factors. It indicates the random factor why people cannot get along well. Thus marriage will not last.

The main hidden stem Xin 辛, a 'Friend' star 比肩星 indicated that this person is strong willed, sincere to friendship, not easily changed, like freedom, resolute, decisive, sincere and truthful, confidence, integrity, careful and patient, independent, brave, cool and steady.

Due to this person concern more of friend than close kin, their marriage is usually problematic.

Note on 'Friend' star 比肩星 :

i) Ren, Gui Water 'Friend' star 水比肩 (壬 癸) folks are 'hasty'. They are rather impatient.

ii) Jia, Yi Wood 'Friend' star 木 比肩 (甲 乙) folks are slow and

105

steady. They will always take their time in whatever they do. They like their spouse to follow their instructions.

iii) Bing, Ding Fire 'Friend' star 火 比肩 (丙 丁) folks are very bashful (they do things without thinking). They like to be informed on everything. They are likely to have children first then marry.

iv) Wu Yi Earth 'Friend' star 土 比肩 (戊己) folks are honest and straight-forward. They do not twist and turn their words. They will say whatever in their minds without regards to the other party feelings;

v) Geng Xin Metal 'Friend' star 金 比肩 (庚辛) folks are firm and unyielding. They will marry whoever they fancy no matter suitable or not.

Folks with this Xin You Day Master 辛酉日元 should not marry young (preferably after 28-year-old), otherwise chance of separation or divorce is very high (due to the 'Friend' star in the main hidden stem).

However, if their 'bone weight' is more than 4 tael 2 mael 骨 4两 2钱, then the chance of separation or divorce is lesser.

Lady with this Day Master must take care of their health, especially gynecological issues 妇科病. The health issues will be more serious if they are obese.

Guy with this Day Master is good if they share their financial management with their (thus they will not squander money on other people. Folks with 'Friend' star usually spent their money on friends rather than their close kin).

*** Folks with Xin You 辛酉末日元 Day Master are likely to meet their future spouse born in the Year or Month of the Rat, Rabbit, Dog, Cockerel 子 兔 狗 鸡 年 月 or when their spouse palace encountered clash, conflict or harm 夫妻宫被审型破害.

XL.viii) Xin Hai Master
辛亥日元:

	Year	Month	Day Master	Hour
Heaven Stem			**Xin** 辛	
Earth Branch			**Hai** 亥	
Hidden Stem			壬-HO 甲 DW	
10 Luck Cycle	3 yo 辛未	13 yo 庚午	23 yo 己巳	33 yo 戊辰	43 yo 丁卯	53 yo 丙寅	63 yo 乙丑	73 yo 甲子	83 yo 癸亥

This Day Pillar is termed "Glittering Pig Day 金光猪日".

This Day Master is ominous as it has the harmful "Lonely Phoenix Calamities star 孤鸾煞" which when activated will cause wife and husband conflicts and quarrels, that resulted in multi-marriage, if not separated or divorced the other party will die first.

The Heaven Stem Xin 辛 Metal produced Branch Hai 亥 Water, indicated this person have cultural skills.

Lady with this Day Master are usually unfaithful (spouse palace Hai 亥 is at the "Bath 沐浴" Stage of life, indicating vanity. She will always scold her husband (due to the present of the Hurting Officer star).

Guy with this Day Master are likely to benefit from wife wealth or have a pretty wife.

Folks with this Xin Hai Day Master 辛亥日元, the gals feelings are likely to feel hurt (physically and mentally). She will withhold her hurt feeling and let it out after her marriage. This is due to the Hurting Officer star at the spouse palace. That's why lady chart with Hurting Officer star will always scold or bully their husband.

Note: Lady with this Day Master will dot the son more (Hurting Officer star is a lady's son star).

After marriage, the wife health will deteriorate especially after childbirth.

If they have a son, it is advised that child don't call the father 'father' (call daddy or uncle), this will break the 'destroying son' hoodoo 克子煞 (that is the son will demise before their parents).

Note: In olden time, folks with this Day Master seldom divorce no matter how they fight or quarrel. But present day are different probably due to western influences?

Lady with this Day Master, when the Hurting Officer star is 'vibrant' it will cause the demise of her husband 伤旺杀夫.

Unfortunately, lady with this Day Master are inflicted with the harmful "Lonely Phoenix Calamities star 孤鸾煞" which when activated will cause wife and husband conflicts and quarrels, that resulted in multi-marriage, if not separated or divorced the other party will die first.

Fortunately, the calamities is the weakest of the "Lonely Phoenix Calamities". As long as their 'bone weight' is more than 4 tael 2 mael and/or don't get marry during the year that conflict with the Year Deity 犯太岁年, they will avoid these calamities.

Folks with this Day Master are usually very filial. But they will easily felt depressed over minor issues (caused by the Hurting Officer star energies).

*** Folks with Xin Hai 辛亥未日元 Day Master are likely to meet their future spouse born in the Year or Month of the Tiger, Snake, Monkey, Pig 虎 蛇 猴 猪 年 月 or when their spouse palace encountered clash, conflict or harm 夫妻宫被审型破害.

Chapter 9 :
Ren Yang Water 壬阳水

Ren Water, a Yang Water is classified as Autumn dew. Ren Water source is Shen 申 Metal. Water produce Wood 水生木.

Ren Water represent vast volume of moving energies such as river and oceans. Thus, Ren Water is blue in color like the vast ocean.

When the 'black cloud' (the Wu Earth) covers the sky, everything will be total darkness, thus Wu Earth 'suppress/destroy' Ren Water.

At Heaven stem it represents the vast sky.

At Earth Branch hidden stem, it represents Water, on earth it represents Sea/Oceans.

Ren Water is represented by the Gan trigram 乾卦 in the Later Heaven 8 Bagua trigrams that represent the Sea/Oceans.

In astrology it represents Uranus planet.

In places, it denotes the river, lake, irrigation canal, tunnel, spring water, road, pathway, subway, doors, prison etc.

In people, it denotes boatman, cavalry, busybody, disreputable women, pregnant women, wet nurse, mother, robber etc.

In emotions/temperament, it denote realistic, pragmatic, slick and sly, intelligent, acute, frank and straight-forward, vague, tolerant, soft but firm internally etc.

In body parts, it denote urinary bladder, oviduct, vas Deren's, ureter, arteries, lymphatic system, mammary glands, lower leg, pregnancy, fetal movement, lower back pain etc.

In things/objects, it denotes transportation, shipbuilding, hydraulic engineering, firefighters, fishery, environment control, deep-freezing, laborer, upright and honest, sexual behavior etc.

In plants/vegetations, it denotes soybean, black bean, ginseng, rubber tree, thorny plants etc.

In animals, it denotes swallow, butterfly, flying fox, rat, owl, walrus, hippopotamus, dolphin, sea urchin, hedgehog etc.

In utensils/instruments, it denotes freezer, air conditioner, boat, water cooler, water pipe, drinking straw, facial cream, hair oil, lubricating oil, lime, dairy products, beverage etc.

XL.ix) Xin Si Master
辛巳日元:

	Year	Month	Day Master	Hour
Heaven Stem			**Ren** 壬	
Earth Branch			Zi 子	
Hidden Stem			癸 - RW	
10 Luck Cycle	3 yo 辛未	13 yo 庚午	23 yo 己巳	33 yo 戊辰	43 yo 丁卯	53 yo 丙寅	63 yo 乙丑	73 yo 甲子	83 yo 癸亥

This Day Pillar is termed "Aquatic Rat Day 水鼠日".

This is a bad Day Master as it has the harmful "Lonely Phoenix Calamities star.
孤鸾煞" which when activated will cause wife and husband conflicts and quarrels, that resulted in multi-marriage, if not separated or divorced the other party will die first.

This Day Master Water energies are too strong indicating this person is handsome/ pretty.

Lady will not take care of household affair. They are usually spendthrift and flirtatious (Zi子 is a Peach Blossom star).

Guy is romantic and flirtatious (Zi子 is a Peach Blossom star). If they make money through their business, they will squander off all the money too (due to the Rob Wealth star present).

Folks with this Ren Zi Day Master 壬子日元 are plagued with Peach Blossom calamities, guy is playboy while gal is 'loose' (due to the strong Peach Blossom star Zi子). Folks with this Day Master are usually well groomed and attractive.

Note: Folks with this Day Master usually have short life as the spouse star Zi子 clashed with Mao卯 and Wu午. Clashes indicated disputes, quarrels disasters. Thus, there will be two months in a year and two out of twelve months there will be troubles. Chart with too many clashes also indicate a short lifespan.

Note: When the Peach Blossom stars shined at the Year and Month pillar, it is known as 'Internal Peach Blossom' where the Peach Blossom is the person caused. These Peach Blossom stars usually indicated this person are very likable and pleasant looking.

When the Peach Blossom stars shined at the Day and Hour pillars, it is known as 'External Peach Blossom' where the affairs involved outsiders (business associates, office colleagues. These affairs usually are extra-marital affairs that will break a happy family.

Folks with this Day Master usually will encounter a 'third party' in their relationships. They will easily have 'secret lover'. This is caused by the romantic nature of the Ren Water Day Master.

Note: Where the spouse palace has 'Friend' star, the chance of separation is very high.

However, where its a Rob Wealth star, the chance of separation or divorce is not so high as long as the couple can understand and care for each other.

Lady with this Day Master are difficult to approach as they are very choosy (due to the Ren Water Day Master). 女人心海底深.

They should educate themselves for future career success (the higher their educations the more successful they will become), due to the Rob Wealth star ('robbing' other people's wealth).

Note: Folks with this Day Master if they have a daughter, they must take very good care of her health. If it's a boy, then no problem.

Besides, this Day Master inflicted the harmful "Lonely Phoenix Calamities star 孤鸾煞" which when activated will cause wife and husband conflicts and quarrels, that resulted in multi-marriage, if not separated or divorced the other party will die first.

*** Folks with Ren Zi Day Master

壬子日元 are likely to meet their future spouse born in the Year or Month of the Rabbit, Horse, Cockerel, Goat 兔 马 鸡 羊 年 月 or when their spouse palace encountered clash, conflict or harm 夫妻宫被审型破害..

L) Ren Yin Day Master 壬寅日元:

	Year	Month	Day Master	Hour
Heaven Stem			**Ren** 壬	
Earth Branch			**Yin** 寅	
Hidden Stem			甲-EG 丙-IW 戊-SK	
10 Luck Cycle	3 yo 辛未	13 yo 庚午	23 yo 己巳	33 yo 戊辰	43 yo 丁卯	53 yo 丙寅	63 yo 乙丑	73 yo 甲子	83 yo 癸亥

This Day Pillar is termed "Aquatic Tiger Day 水虎日".

This is an auspicious Day Master indicating this person likely to be wealthy and reputable. Heaven stem Ren Water produced Branch Yin Wood, indicating a blissful family.

Folks with this Ren Yin Day Master 壬寅日元 are very hasty and bashful (due to the Eating God star at the main hidden stem). It will cause the woman health especially after birth (Day master produces Eating God star diminishing its energies).

Note: Folks with Indirect Wealth star in their chart are very business minded. Since Wealth star produces Authority stars, they are likely to attain high position in their career.

They will place priority in their career rather than care for the family.

However, Indirect Wealth star suppress Resource stars indicating they do not respect their seniors, including their parents.

When the Seven Killing star shined at the auxiliary hidden stem, it indicated this person will keep all their problems and worries to themselves.

However, when it is 'revealed' at the Heaven Stem, they are easily manipulated as their feelings are shown on their face.

Guy with this Day Master usually are unable to forget their ex-lover, they will secretly care and assist them (due to the Indirect Wealth star which is the guy 'lover'; Seven Killing star which is the gal 'lover' stars influences).

Lady with this Day Master are usually good housewife. They will tend to every household thing with care and completion.

*** Folks with Ren Yin Day Master 壬寅日元 are likely to meet their future spouse born in the Year or Month of the Snake, Monkey, Pig 蛇 猴 猪 年 月 or when their spouse palace encountered clash, conflict or harm 夫妻宫被审型破害.

L.i) Ren Chen Day Master 壬辰日元:

	Year	Month	Day Master	Hour
Heaven Stem			**Ren** 壬	
Earth Branch			**Chen** 辰	
Hidden Stem			戊-SK 乙-HO 癸-RW	
10 Luck Cycle	3 yo 辛未	13 yo 庚午	23 yo 己巳	33 yo 戊辰	43 yo 丁卯	53 yo 丙寅	63 yo 乙丑	73 yo 甲子	83 yo 癸亥

This Day Pillar is termed "Aquatic Dragon Day 水龙日".

This Day Master have the harmful "Freak Error Calamities star" which denotes errors due to chance or random factors. It indicates the random factor why people cannot get along well. Thus, marriage will not last.

Folks with this Day Master born on Hai hour 亥时 are likely to be reputable; Born on Wu hour 午时 likely to lost everything.

Folks with this Ren Chen Day Master 壬辰日元 are inflicted with the "Kui Gang star calamities 魁罡星" which denote limits, things that is out of reach, that always fluctuating. However, these individuals are brave, passionate and chivalrous.

Guy with this Day Master are unable to control their temper. Thus, their marriage life is always problematic (Seven Killing and Hurting Officers stars are ominous stars that bring troubles).

However, these folks are perfectionist.

Lady with this Day Master are likely lived their old age in loneliness (due to the Kui Gang star influence).

Note: All three hidden stem stars are harmful to a lady life.

*** Folks with Ren Chen Day Master 壬辰日元 are likely to meet their future spouse born in the Year or Month of the Cow, Rabbit, Dragon, Dog 牛兔龙狗年月 or when their spouse palace encountered clash, conflict or harm 夫妻宫被审型破害.

L.ii) Ren Wu Day Master 壬午日元:

	Year	Month	Day Master	Hour
Heaven Stem			**Ren** 壬	
Earth Branch			**Wu** 午	
Hidden Stem			丁-DW 己-DA	
10 Luck Cycle	3 yo 辛未	13 yo 庚午	23 yo 己巳	33 yo 戊辰	43 yo 丁卯	53 yo 丙寅	63 yo 乙丑	73 yo 甲子	83 yo 癸亥

This Day Pillar is termed "Aquatic Horse Day 水马日".

This Day Master Heaven stem and Branch clashed, indicating a problematic marriage life.

The spouse palace have Direct Wealth and Direct Authority stars, indicating this person is likely a upright high ranking official. It also indicated this person will likely have the support of the wife.

Lady is likely to have a faithful and caring husband (Ding Fire merged with Ren Water to transform into a Wood energies).

Folks with this auspicious Ren Wu Day Master 壬午日元 are upright and honorable people that will hold high power position (when these hidden stems are 'useful gods 喜用神'.

They usually bring luck and wealth to their spouse. However, they must avoid the Peach Blossom calamities at all costs (Wu午 is one of the four strong Peach Blossom star).

Note: Direct Authority star are clashed away by the Hurting Officer star (Ren Water Hurting Officer star is Bing Fire), indicating they will lose their job or position) as well being 'combined' away. In the above case, Yi 已 Earth merged with Jia Wood to transform into an Earth energies.

Note: In a chart when there are Direct Authority star as well as Seven Killing stars, it will create a turbulent environment, indicating plenty of disputes and disagreements 官杀混查.

*** Folks with Ren Wu Day Master

壬午日元 are likely to meet their future spouse born in the Year or Month of the Rat, Cow, Rabbit, Horse 鼠 牛 兔 马 年 月 or when their spouse palace encountered clash, conflict or harm 夫妻宫被审型破害.

L.iii) Ren Shen Day Master
壬申日元:

	Year	Month	Day Master	Hour
Heaven Stem			**Ren** 壬	
Earth Branch			**Shen** 申	
Hidden Stem			庚-IR 壬-Fr 戊-SK	
10 Luck Cycle	3 yo 辛未	13 yo 庚午	23 yo 己巳	33 yo 戊辰	43 yo 丁卯	53 yo 丙寅	63 yo 乙丑	73 yo 甲子	83 yo 癸亥	

This Day Pillar is termed "Aquatic Monkey Day 水猴日".

This Day Master had the harmful "The 10 Abomination Defeat 十恶大败" that is a very ominous star that bring disappointments and disasters. "10 Abomination" （十恶） meant unpardonable serious crimes; "Defeat" （大败） meant nothing left (money, food etc.) totally eliminated.

Folks with this Day Master are usually very active and can't control themself.

Males are brave and like to fight thus unlikely to have a peaceful death.

Lady is manly and also like to fight. Folks with this Ren Shen Day Master 壬申日元 have their own way of thinking and doing things (due to the Indirect Resource star). These folks are suitable to be policeman or court judges.

The 'Friend' star will cause different of opinions thus disagreements and disputes aplenty thus separation or divorce is inadvertent. Coupled with the Indirect Resource star energies, they are very strong headed and will not listen to their spouse.

Seven Killing star will cause hasty actions which will be regretted later. If the Seven Killing star are 'revealed', it indicated a period of serious sickness or disaster.

Thus, folks with this Day Master are unlikely to stay together for long.

*** Folks with Ren Shen Day Master 壬申日元 are likely to meet their future spouse born in the Year or Month of the Tiger, Snake, Pig 虎 蛇 猪 年 月 or when their spouse palace encountered clash, conflict or harm 夫妻宫被审型破害.

L.iv) Ren Xu Day Master 壬戌日元:

	Year	Month	Day Master	Hour
Heaven Stem			**Ren** 壬	
Earth Branch			**Xu** 戌	
Hidden Stem			戊-SK 辛-DR 丁-DW	
10 Luck Cycle	3 yo 辛未	13 yo 庚午	23 yo 己巳	33 yo 戊辰	43 yo 丁卯	53 yo 丙寅	63 yo 乙丑	73 yo 甲子	83 yo 癸亥

This Day Pillar is termed "Aquatic Dog Day水狗日".

This Day Master had the harmful "Freak Error Calamities star" which denotes errors due to chance or random factors. It indicate the random factor why people cannot get along well. Thus marriage will not last.

This Day Master also had the "Seven Killing Direct Resource star mutual producing energies which strengthen the Day Master thus indicating this person are likely to be successful in life
坐下财生杀，杀生印，杀印相生，主大贵.

Note: Ding Fire merged with Ren Water to transform into a Earth energies, indicated this person are likely to become a villain or a nasty person.

Folks with this Ren Xu Day Master壬戌日元 have very strong orthodox motivation energies (Seven Killing star aggressiveness are diverted to orthodox energies influenced by the Direct Resource and Direct Wealth stars). Thus, these folks are very law abiding.

Direct Resource star folks are very charitable and caring.

Direct Wealth star folks are family oriented and will take care of their family welfare. Their home is always well maintained and tidy.

Guy with this Day Master need to settled down first before they can have success in their career or business (Direct Wealth star at the auxiliary stem).

Note: Folks with this Day Master are likely to encounter problems at the age of 9, 19, 29, 39, 49, 59, 69 and so on....(nine is the transition age when their star cross over from one palace to another, such as then the Year Branch crossed over to the Month stem; the Month Branch crossed over to the Day Stem; Day Branch crossed over to the Hour stem).

Lady with this Day Master will love her husband as well as take good care of the family affairs, they are good housewife.

However, they must be wary of her husband social life as he may have 'secret' lover.

*** Folks with Ren Xu Day Master 壬戌日元 are likely to meet their future spouse born in the Year or Month of the Cow, Dragon, Goat, Cockerel 牛 龙 羊 鸡 年 or when their spouse palace encountered clash, conflict or harm 夫妻宫被审型破害.

Chapter 10 :
Gui Yin Water 癸 阴水

Gui癸Water is Yin Water阴水.

At Heaven stem it denote Rain, Dew, Snow.

At Earth hidden stem it denote spring water, thus is a Yin Water, a flowing water, gentle and soft.

Gui Water are produced by Metal. Frozen Metal will produce dew (which is Water). At the same time, dew(water) nourish plants, thus Gui Water produce Yi Wood.

In astrology it is the Neptune planet. In places, it denote ocean, peninsula, mass of water, water well, toilet, cellar, depot, warehouse, prison, back door, exit, escape route etc.

In people, it denote doctor, hermit, psychologist, surveyor, diver, detective, spy, drunkard, young child, beggar etc.

In emotions/temperament, it denotes honest and straight-forward, sentimental, cherish old friendships, uncommunicative, secretive etc.

In body parts, it denotes kidney, reproductive system, nervous system, ears, brain, bones, limbs, equilibrium system, memory, saliva etc.

In things/objects, it denotes staff officer, dispatcher, scheduler, plan, design, survey, plot, flee, wedding day, lost, hoard etc.

In plants/vegetations, it denotes plum blossom, narcissus, camellia, snow lotus herb, ningo figwort, asparagus, dwarf lilyturf, algae etc.

In animals, it denotes penguin, otter, polar bear, sable, marten, pig, oyster, abalone, mew gull, tadpole etc.

In utensils/instruments, it denotes spirit leveler, water filter, conical bamboo hat, writing materials, joss paper money, detergent etc.

L.v) Gui Chou Day Master 癸丑日元:

	Year	Month	Day Master	Hour
Heaven Stem			**Gui** 癸	
Earth Branch			**Chou** 丑	
Hidden Stem			己-SK 癸-Fr 辛-IR	
10 Luck Cycle	3 yo 辛未	13 yo 庚午	23 yo 己巳	33 yo 戊辰	43 yo 丁卯	53 yo 丙寅	63 yo 乙丑	73 yo 甲子	83 yo 癸亥

This Day Pillar is termed "Rain Cow Day 雨牛日".

This Day Master sat on its own 'wealth depository 坐财库 thus during the Current Cycle or 10 Year Luck Cycle when their Day Master energies are strengthened, this person will become wealthy.

Folks with this Gui Chou Day Master 癸丑日元 (having the 'Friend' star' revealed') prefer partner to have many views but after marriage they are likely to be separated or divorce due to differences in their views and thinking). "Friend" star together with Seven Killing stars energies 杀比同宫.

Lady with this Day Master, after their marriage, they will render much support and sacrifices to their in-laws ('Friend' star 'letting' Seven Killing star took main hidden stem position). Also indicated this lady couldn't save money 杀生偏印.

Note: Chart with an Earth Element need Water Element to make it useful (Earth Element without Water are 'rock', thus is useless as it could not support any plant/vegetations, i.e., could not support grow).

*** Folks with Gui Chou Day Master 癸丑日元 are likely to meet their future spouse born in the Year or Month of the Dragon, Horse, Goat, Dog 龙 马 羊 狗 年 or when their spouse palace encountered clash, conflict or harm 夫妻宫被审型破害..

L.vi) Gui Mao Day Master 癸卯日元:

	Year	Month	Day Master	Hour
Heaven Stem			**Gui** 癸	
Earth Branch			**Mao** 卯	
Hidden Stem			乙 - EG	
10 Luck Cycle	3 yo 辛未 / 13 yo 庚午 / 23 yo 己巳 / 33 yo 戊辰	43 yo 丁卯	53 yo 丙寅 / 63 yo 乙丑	73 yo 甲子 / 83 yo 癸亥

This Day Pillar is termed "Rain Rabbit Day 雨兔日".

The spouse star Mao卯 a Peach Blossom star, indicated spouse are romantic and flirtatious.

Main hidden stem Yi乙 an Eating God star, indicated this person will have plentiful of foods and entertainment. Also indicated this person is intelligent and have good literary skills.

Lady with this Day Master likely to have a well-educated son.

Folks with this Gui Mao Day Master癸卯日元 will not worry about their daily needs (Eating God star 食神星 bring plentiful foods and joy)

Gui Water produced Mao Wood.

When the Eating God star is an "useful god 喜用神", it must not be clashed or suppressed otherwise it will be disastrous, especially when there's an Indirect Resource star (which will suppress/destroy the Eating God star).

However, when the Eating God star is the main hidden stem, it indicated this individual health are not good (Eating God stars are produced by the Day Master thus snapping its energies causing poor health, especially mother after giving birth).

When the Eating God stars are 'revealed' it indicated these individuals will attain success in their career or business. But they must not overindulgence in foods and drinks (too much will affect their health).

These folks should settle down young and start a family. They will have a happy family and children will be filial. Lady with this Day Master better to have a husband older than themselves this is because their husband is likely to be carefree and cannot control what he is doing, thus need the wife to supervise his behaviors and doings.

*** Folks with Gui Mao Day Master 癸卯日元 are likely to meet their future spouse born in the Year or Month of the Tiger, Monkey, Pig 虎 猴 猪 年 月 or when their spouse palace encountered clash, conflict or harm 夫妻宫被审型破害.

L.vii) Gui Si Day Master 癸巳日元:

	Year	Month	Day Master	Hour
Heaven Stem			**Gui** 癸	
Earth Branch			**Si** 巳	
Hidden Stem			丙 - DW 戊 - DA 庚 - DR	
10 Luck Cycle	3 yo 辛未	13 yo 庚午	23 yo 己巳	33 yo 戊辰	43 yo 丁卯	53 yo 丙寅	63 yo 乙丑	73 yo 甲子	83 yo 癸亥

This Day Pillar is termed "Rain Snake Day 雨蛇日".

This is a very ominous Day Master. It had the harmful "Lonely Phoenix Calamities star 孤鸾煞" which when activated will cause wife and husband conflicts and quarrels, that resulted in multi-marriage, if not separated or divorced the other party will die first..

As well as the harmful "Freak Error Calamities star" which denotes errors due to chance or random factors. It indicates the random factor why people cannot get along well. Thus, marriage will not last.

Lady are likely to marry a good and caring husband (due to the present of Direct Authority, Direct Wealth and Direct Resource stars, all very auspicious stars).

Folks with this Gui Si Day Master 癸巳日元 are usually upright, orthodox excellent employee.

All the 'Direct' stars indicated they will be successful in management and likely to be a high position authoritative officer such as a court judge, company CEO or Departmental head.

Guy with this Day Master usually are good husband. They will take good are of his family and usually faithful.

But they should not venture into business as there is no Indirect Wealth stars, indicating they do not have business acumen and not adventurous.

Lady with this Day Master are considered beneficial to her as she will give her full support and assistances to ensure her husband success. Some divination master considered her to be 'benefactor 贵人' but is wrong. 'Benefactor 贵人' are people to come to one's aids during time of needs.

*** Folks with Gui Si Day Master
癸巳日元 are likely to meet their future spouse born in the Year or Month of the Tiger, Monkey, Pig 虎 猴 猪 年 月 or when their spouse palace encountered clash, conflict or harm 夫妻宫被审型破害.

L.viii) Gui Wei Day Master 癸未日元:

	Year	Month	Day Master	Hour
Heaven Stem			**Gui** 癸	
Earth Branch			**Wei** 未	
Hidden Stem			己 - SK 丁 - IW 乙 - EG	
10 Luck Cycle	3 yo 辛未	13 yo 庚午	23 yo 己巳	33 yo 戊辰	43 yo 丁卯	53 yo 丙寅	63 yo 乙丑	73 yo 甲子	83 yo 癸亥

This Day Pillar is termed "Rain Goat Day 雨羊日".

This Day Master have the auspicious "Ten Efficacious Day 十灵日" energies that indicate this person is clever and quick-witted. When this Day Master encountered the Gui Wei癸未 during the Current Cycle or 10 Year Luck Cycle, this person will remarry. As they are romantic and flirtatious, their married life won't last long.

Folks with this Gui Wei Day Master 癸未日元 guy have high expectations of his wife and very selective. Furthermore, after marriage he is likely to be involved in extra-marital affairs.

The Seven Killing star also indicated this person is a troublemaker. Thus their marriage usually will not last. However, if they placed their aggressiveness in their work, they will be very successful.

Lady with this Day Master will always remember their ex-lover or the one that hurt her feeling most (a weird behavior).   These ladies usually will get the attention of their date (fatal attractions).

They are likely to get facial makeover or body shaping courses.

Note: In ancient texts, lady with this Day Master if they are attractive look, usually they have short life

Folks with this Day Master must be able to find their Peach Blossom palace, otherwise they will find it difficult to meet their future spouse. Energizing the Peach Blossom palace will increase a person's affinities and good public relationships. However, Peach Blossom energies after marriage is bad as it bring 'external affairs' that will break up a family.

*** Folks with Gui Wei Day Master 癸未日元 are likely to meet their future spouse born in the Year or Month of the Rat, Cow, Dog 鼠 牛 狗 年 月 or when their spouse palace encountered clash, conflict or harm 夫妻宫被审型破害.

L.ix) Gui You Day Master 癸酉日元:

	Year	Month	Day Master	Hour
Heaven Stem			**Gui** 癸	
Earth Branch			**You** 酉	
Hidden Stem			辛 - IR	
10 Luck Cycle	3 yo 辛未	13 yo 庚午	23 yo 己巳	33 yo 戊辰	43 yo 丁卯	53 yo 丙寅	63 yo 乙丑	73 yo 甲子	83 yo 癸亥

This Day Pillar is termed "Rain Cockerel Day 雨鸡日".

The main hidden stem, a Indirect Resource star indicated this person looked gentle externally but have an evil heart. Folks with this Gui You Day Master 癸酉日元 guy does not like other to interfere with his family affairs (Indirect Resource star energies).

Indirect Resource stars will create uncontrollable reactions which the person will regret later. Folks with Indirect Resource star are usually introvert, moody and unapproachable.

Guy with this Day Master, as their spouse palace sat this You酉 star, it indicated the wife have good oral and vocal skills, thus likely to be a lecturer or a singer.

Note: These guys are unlikely to attain high authority positive (Indirect Resource star suppressed/destroyed Authority stars)

Lady with this Day Master will frequently face disasters (Indirect Resource stars suppress/destroy Eating God stars, indicating her joy and enjoyments will be destroyed). Thus, they usually are loner and can't get along with other people.

Even if they are married, she will not stay with the in-laws. They do not believe in getting registered for their marriage, just marry not need to register.

Note: It is good for her to marry a guy whom chart has Direct Authority star (which is her husband star), thus her marriage will be good.

*** Folks with Gui You Day Master 癸酉日元 are likely to meet their future spouse born in the Year or Month of the Rat, Rabbit, Dog, cockerel 鼠 兔 狗 鸡 年 月 or when their spouse palace encountered clash, conflict or harm 夫妻宫被审型破害.

LX) Gui You Day Master 癸酉日元:

	Year	Month	Day Master	Hour
Heaven Stem			Gui 癸	
Earth Branch			Hai 亥	
Hidden Stem			壬 - RW 甲 - HO	
10 Luck Cycle	3 yo 辛未	13 yo 庚午	23 yo 己巳	33 yo 戊辰	43 yo 丁卯	53 yo 丙寅	63 yo 乙丑	73 yo 甲子	83 yo 癸亥

This Day Pillar is termed "Rain Pig Day 雨猪日".

This Day Master had the harmful "Freak Error Calamities star" which denotes errors due to chance or random factors. It indicates the random factor why people cannot get along well. Thus, marriage will not last.

This Day Master also sat on the "Star of Goat Blade 羊刃星" which is the Branch' Rob Wealth star 劫才星.

This Star represent a fierce and powerful force of disaster and calamities. This person will likely take the law unto themselves. They are unlikely to have a peaceful death.

Folks with this Gui Hai Day Master 癸亥日元, as the main hidden stem is the Rob Wealth star 劫才星, their attitude towards their partner are bad.

They always deem all issues arise from the other partner (Rob Wealth star are the negative mirror image of their own characters).

Note: Rob Wealth star frequently caused the person to have good affection/ feeling towards similar sex people (thus the likelihood of being gay is quite high).

This Day Master have Rob Wealth and Hurting Officer (especially when they are ominous 忌神）stars in the same palace, indicated they are likely to be cheated by friends as well as they are gamblers. In worst case, they may be landed in prison.

Note: i) A strong Day Master will neutralize the harmful effects of the Hurting Officer star, thus will be able to benefit from wife support/caring.

ii) The Authority stars will suppress/control the Rob Wealth star.

*** Folks with Gui Hai Day Master 癸亥日元 are likely to meet their future spouse born in the Year or Month of the Tiger, Snake, Monkey, Pig 虎 蛇 申 猪 年 月 or when their spouse palace encountered clash, conflict or harm 夫妻宫被审型破害.

Chapter 11 : Peach Blossom

Since this book discussed Marriage and Relationships, it also concerns the Peach Blossom star. There are many methods to determine the Peach Blossom star palaces/locations.

i) From the main door directions.
ii) From the Day Master Wealth (for male), Authority star (for lady).
iii) From the Day Master spouse palace.
iv) From Year of birth.
v) From natal chart Year and/or Day Branch.

i) From the main door directions:

The direction opposite the main door direction is the person Peach Blossom palace. These position can magnify the Peach Blossom energies to enhance one's chance of meeting the future spouse as well as to help in one's career of those in the entertainment and networking industries.

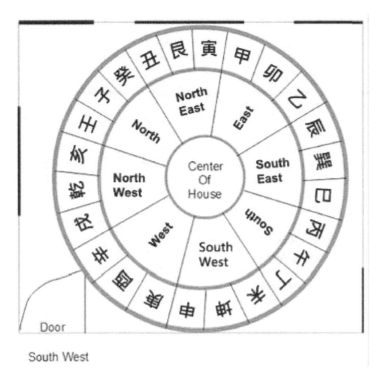

South West

In above example, the main door is facing South West, so the Peach Blossom direction is North East and the Peach Blossom stars are Chou 丑, Gen 艮, Yin 寅 (see table below):

Door Facing Direction	Peach Blossom **Direction**	Peach Blossom **Palace**
North	South	丙 午 丁
North East	South West	未 坤 申
East	West	庚 酉 辛
South East	North West	戌 乾 亥
South	North	壬 子 癸
South West	North East	丑 艮 寅
West	East	甲 卯 乙
North West	South East	辰 巽 巳

ii) From the Day Master Wealth (for male) / Authority star (for lady):

    Checking from the Day Master Branch (the person spouse palace), the Element that it suppressed/controlled is deemed the Peach Blossom Year and Month (see chart below);

    Male destiny refer their Wealth stars when they are "useful star 喜用神";

    Female destiny refer their Authority stars when they are "useful star 喜用神" :

	Year	Month	Day Master	Hour
Heaven Stem			**Gui** 癸	
Earth Branch			**Mao** 卯	
Hidden Stem			乙 - EG	
10 Luck Cycle	3 yo 辛未	13 yo 庚午	23 yo 己巳	33 yo 戊辰	43 yo 丁卯	53 yo 丙寅	63 yo 乙丑	73 yo 甲子	83 yo 癸亥

Day Master Gui 癸 Water suppressed/ controlled Wu 戊 Earth, so Wu 戊 Year and Wu 戊 Month are this person Peach Blossom Year and Month (see chart below):

Day Branch (Day born)	Peach Blossom Year	Peach Blossom Month
Jia Wood 甲木	Yi Earth Year 己土年	Yi Earth Month 己土月
Yi Wood 乙木	Geng Metal Year 庚金年	Geng Metal Month 庚金月
Bing Fire 丙火	Xin Metal Year 辛金年	Xin Metal Month 辛金月
Ding Fire 丁火	Ren Water Year 壬水年	Ren Water Month 壬水月
Wu Earth 戊土	Gui Water Year 癸水年	Gui Water Month 癸水月
Yi Earth 己土	Jia Wood Year 甲木年	Jia Wood Month 甲木月
Geng Earth 庚金	Yi Wood Year 乙木年	Yi Wood Month 乙木月
Xin Earth 辛金	Bing Fire Year 丙火年	Bing Fire Month 丙火月
Ren Water 壬	Ding Fire Year 丁火年	Ding Fire Month 丁火月
Gui Water 癸	Wu Earth Year 戊土年	Wu Earth Month 戊土月

spouse palace:

Refering to the spouse palace, the Peach Blossom stars will appear as follow:

Spouse Palace star	Peach Blossom star will appear in these Year or Month or when clashed
Yin 寅	Snake, Monkey, Pig 蛇 猴 猪 年 月
Mao 卯	Tiger, Monkey, Pig 虎 猴 猪 年 月
Chen 辰	Cow, Rabbit, Dragon, Dog 牛 兔 龙 狗 年 月
Si 巳	Tiger, Monkey, Pig 虎 猴 猪 年 月
Wu 午	Rat, Cow, Rabbit, Horse 鼠 牛 兔 马 年 月
Wei 未	Rat, Cow, Dog 鼠 牛 狗 年 月
Shen 申	Tiger, Snake, Pig 虎 蛇 猪 年 月
You 酉	Rat, Rabbit, Dog or Cockerel 子 卯 狗 鸡 年 月
Xu 戌	Cow, Dragon, Goat, Cockerel 牛 龙 羊 鸡 年 月
Hai 亥	Tiger, Snake, Monkey, Pig 虎 蛇 申 猪 年 月
Zi 子	Rabbit, Horse, Cockerel, Goat 兔 马 鸡 羊 年 月
Chou 丑	Dragon, Horse, Goat, Dog 龙 马 羊 狗 年 月

Example: If the spouse palace is Wu午 then this person will encounter their Peach Blossom star in the Year or Month of the Rat, Cow, Rabbit, Horse.

	Year	Month	Day Master	Hour
Heaven Stem	Yi 乙			
Earth Branch	Wei 未			
Hidden Stem	己-IW 丁-EG 乙-Fr			

This person is born in the Year of the Goat 未年生, thus their Peach Blossom will appear in the direction at North (refer to chart below):

Year of birth			Peach Blossom Direction
Rat 鼠	Dragon 龙	Monkey 猴	West
Tiger 虎	Horse 马	Dog 狗	East
Snake 蛇	Cockerel 鸡	Cow 牛	South
Pig 猪	Rabbit 兔	Goat 羊	North

Year of Birth
Peach Blossom Direction

Tiger Year 虎年		Rabbit Year 兔年	
Geng Yin 庚寅	1950, 2010	Xin Mao 辛卯	1951, 2011
Ren Yin 壬寅	1962, 2012	Gui Mao 癸卯	1963, 2023
Jia Yin 甲寅	1974, 2024	Yi Mao 乙卯	1975, 2035
Bing Yin 丙寅	1986, 2036	Ding Mao 丁卯	1987, 2047
Wu Yin 戊寅	1998, 2042	Yi Mao 已卯	1999, 2059

Dragon Year 龙年		Snake Year 蛇年	
Ren Chen 壬辰	1952, 2012	Gui Si 癸巳	1953, 2013
Jia Chen 甲辰	1964, 2024	Yi Si 乙巳	1965, 2025
Bing Chen 丙辰	1976, 2036	Ding Si 丁巳	1977, 2037
Wu Chen 戊辰	1988, 2048	Yi Si 乙巳	1989, 2049
Geng Chen 庚辰	2000, 2060	Xin Si 辛巳	2001, 2061

Horse Year 马 年		Goat Year 羊 年	
Jia Wu 甲午	1954, 2014	Yi Wei 乙未	1955, 2015
Bing Wu 丙午	1966, 2026	Ding Wei 丁未	1967, 2027
Wu Wu 戊午	1978, 2038	Yi Wei 己未	1979, 2039
Geng Wu 庚午	1990, 2050	Geng Wei 庚未	1991, 2051
Ren Wu 壬午	2002, 2062	Gui Wei 癸未	2003, 2063

Monkey Year 猴 年		Cockerel Year 鸡 年	
Bing Shen 丙申	1956, 2016	Ding You 丁酉	1957, 2017
Wu Shen 戊申	1968, 2028	Yi You 己酉	1969, 2029
Geng Shen 庚申	1980, 2040	Xin You 辛酉	1981, 2041
Ren Shen 壬申	1992, 2052	Gui You 癸酉	1993, 2053
Jia Shen 甲申	2004, 2064	Yi You 乙酉	2005, 2065

Dog Year 狗 年		Pig Year 猪 年	
Wu Xu 戊戌	1958, 2018	Yi Hai 己亥	1959, 2019
Geng Xu 庚戌	1970, 2030	Xin Hai 辛亥	1971, 2031
Ren Xu 壬戌	1982, 2042	Gui Hai 癸亥	1983, 2043
JiaXu 甲戌	1994, 2054	Yi Hai 乙亥	1995, 2055
Bing Xu 丙戌	2006, 2066	Ding Hai 丁亥	2007, 2067

Rat Year 鼠 年		Cow Year 牛 年	
Geng Zi 庚子	1960, 2020	Xin Chou 辛丑	1961, 2021
Ren Zi 壬子	1972, 2032	Gui Chou 癸丑	1973, 2033
Jia Zi 甲子	1984, 2044	Yi Chou 乙丑	1985, 2045
Bing Zi 丙子	1996, 2056	Ding Chou 丁丑	1997, 2057
Wu Zi 戊子	2008, 2068	Yi Chou 己丑	2009, 2069

v) From natal chart Year and/or Day Branch :

Year/Day Branch	Yin 寅	Wu 午	Xu 戌	Shen 申	Zi 子	Chen 辰	Hai 亥	Mao 卯	Wei 未	Si 巳	You 酉	Chou 丑
Any Branch	Mao 卯			You 酉			Zi 子			Wu 午		
Star of Romance (Peach Blossom Star) 桃花												

    Peach Blossom stars influence the emotion, desire, charisma and marriage of an individual.

    Peach Blossom star influence the emotion, desire, charisma and marriage of an individual.

Since anciently, the Peach Blossom star are associated with the sexual desires of men and women. It refers to the good and bad social relationship between people. It also indicated the good look and appeal.

Chart with this Star indicate inclination to have much better social interaction than those without. Thus the competent use of this Star shall generate beneficial social relationship, which can reap exceptional rewards.

Male individual with many Direct Wealth 正财星 and Indirect Wealth 偏才星 will surely have Peach Blossom situations.

For Male, Direct Wealth star represent wife; Indirect Wealth star represent his 'lover'.

For Female, Direct Authority star represent the husband; Seven Killing star (Indirect Authority star) represent her 'lover'.

Female with this Star in their Chart will attract the attention of the opposite sex. Even if married, they will have extra-martial affair with other men, thus likely to cause problem in family life. For Female, Direct Authority star represent husband; Seven Killing star represent her 'lover'.

When this Star appeared on top of the Indirect Wealth star (偏才星) or at the Year or Month Stem, this person' father is rather romantic (Indirect Wealth star represent the father).

When this Star appeared on top of the 'Friend and/or Rob Wealth Stars (比肩星, 劫才星), it represents a Peach Blossom calamity (such as separation or even divorce).

When this Star appeared on top of the Seven Killing Star (七杀星), this person is likely to be womanizer and a drinker.

Female with Direct Officer star (正官星) on top of Peach Blossom star will likely marry a rich guy, however the husband is also likely to have a mistress.

When there's a Peach Blossom star in the chart and there's a Zi Mao clash (子卯冲), the individual will have a strong attraction for the opposite sex, thus will cause a disastrous family life (such as separation or divorce).

Female with a Peach Blossom star in their chart and when there's Direct Authority star 正官星 and Seven Killing star 七杀星, marriage is likely to break down (Seven Killing star destroy the Direct Authority star which is her husband star).

The Peach Blossom Star is determined with the Year or Day Branch as focus, when it encounter any of the following Earth Branch, is deemed as the "Peach Blossom Star 桃花星"

Example:

	Year	Month	Day Master	Hour
Heaven Stem	Yi 己		Jia 甲	
Earth Branch	Hai 亥		Zi 子	
Hidden Stem	壬-DA 甲-DW		癸-DR	

In the above example, the Year Stem is Hai亥, so during the Current Year or 10 Year Cycle when it encountered Zi子, the Peach Blossom star appeared, indicating this person will meet their future spouse or likely a marriage year if there's a combination or clashes of the spouse palace.

Note: The Day Branch is Zi子, it indicated:

i) this person likely to meet their future spouse after the age of 37 year old;

ii) this is also the person spouse palace, indicating the spouse is very likable and romantic.

Furthermore, during the Current Year or 10 Year Cycle when it encountered You酉, the Peach Blossom star appeared, indicating this person will meet their future spouse or likely a marriage year if there's an combination or clashes of the spouse palace.

Conclusion

All humans are influenced by affection and feeling, thus the important of the Peach Bossom stars and location.

A knowledge of your Peach Blossom stars and locations goes a long way in improving a person's lifestyle and destiny.

Know your Peach Blossom stars and locations and be a better person.

If you wish to know when you will likely meet your future spouse or when you will get married, get a free Bazi destiny reading.

Send your Year, Month, Day and Hour to: If you have a Chinese name, include your Chinese characters):

patkong2657@gmail.com

Made in the USA
Las Vegas, NV
06 October 2023